Rudolf Baumbach

RUDOLPH BAUMBACH'S
TALES

TRANSLATED FROM THE GERMAN

BY

HELEN B. DOLE

NEW YORK
THOMAS Y. CROWELL & CO.
PUBLISHERS

TYPOGRAPHY BY J. S. CUSHING & Co.

ISBN 13: 978-1-4344-8386-7

TRANSLATOR'S PREFACE.

RUDOLPH BAUMBACH is a poet. He was born in Thuringia, and now lives in Leipsic, where he is a favorite both as a writer and in society. Most of his works have been written in verse, which is spontaneous, full of melody, and as witty as Heine, but perfectly free from bitterness. He draws his inspiration largely from the Alps. His "Zlatorog," an Alpine story, has reached the twenty-second edition, and the "Lieder eines fahrenden Gesellen" and "Frau Holde" are each in the thirteenth edition.

The present collection of short stories has been taken from two little volumes in prose, entitled, "Sommer-Märchen" and "Erzählungen und Mär-chen," which have been very popular in Germany. More than eleven editions of the first volume have been sold, and six of the second. They have also been published with handsome illustrations by Paul Mohn. The stories are remarkable for their grace and simplicity of style. They are full of originality and wit, with occasional touches of keen satire, showing knowledge of the world as well as a familiarity with every bird and flower and creature in forest, field, and mountain. The stories are more for young people than children, yet the " Easter Rabbit " will be enjoyed by the little ones, while the fun in the " Ass's Spring " will appeal to children of a larger growth. They are not altogether fairy-tales, though all border on the marvellous, and sprites, elves, and other mysterious folk from Wonderland play a conspicuous part.

HELEN B. DOLE.

BOSTON, April 18, 1888.

CONTENTS.

PROLOGUE.

My gallant courser swift and good
   Through story-land conveys me;
The mystic lady of the wood
   With runic staff delays me;
The water-nissie sings her lays
   Beside the fairy fountain;
The golden-antlered white stag plays
   In sunlight on the mountain.

Deep down in caverns I behold
   Brown kobolds evil scheming;
I see their hoards of hidden gold
   Like coals of red fire gleaming.
The speech of birds and beasts I know,
   The lore of trees and flowers;
I use all magic herbs that grow —
   Their good and evil powers.

To join his midnight gallop wild
  The Huntsman oft invites me;
Upon the moonlit meadows mild
  The Elfin dance delights me;
The gray-haired witch upon her fire
  A cheering draught can brew me;
The crested dragon calms his ire,
  And fawning grovels to me.

My courser starts, and whinnies clear;
  He spurns the Earth's dominions;
Upon his shoulders broad appear
  Two spreading snow-white pinions.
Swift as the storm, away we fly
  Through measureless expanses —
Ah no! at home in bed I lie
  And dream my pleasant fancies.

RANUNCULUS, THE MEADOW SPRITE.

ONCE upon a time there was a young school-master who, in spite of his youth, was so wise and learned that when the seven wise men of Greece, during a visit to the upper world, held a disputation with him, they stood like dunces before him.

This same schoolmaster started out into the fields, one spring morning, to hear the grass grow; for he knew all about that too. And as he wandered through the bright green mead-ows, and saw the variegated marvels of the air flying around the star-flowers, and heard the crickets in the grass, the birds in the branches, and the frogs in the meadow brook, singing their wedding songs, then he thought of his native village, which he had left years before, to go to college, and he thought, too, of the little black-eyed lassie who had given him a

gingerbread heart, as a farewell present, and
shed bitter tears over it; and a strange feeling
came over him.

On the following day the schoolmaster tied
up his bundle, took his knotted staff in his
hand, and started forth, with joy and happiness in his heart, out of the city, into the
green world.

Three days after, he caught a glimpse,
through the blossoming fruit-trees, of the blue
slate-covered roof of his own village church
tower, and the wind brought the mellow sound
of bells to his ears.

"I wonder if she will know me," he said to
himself. "Hardly; and I, too, shall have difficulty to find, in the eighteen-year-old girl, the
little Greta of former days. But her eyes, her
big black eyes, they must betray her to me.
And if I see her sitting by her door, on the
stone bench, I will step up to her side, and —
and the rest will come of itself."

The schoolmaster threw his hat into the air,
and shouted so loud that he was frightened at
his own voice. He looked shyly about him to
see if anybody had witnessed his unruliness; but,
except a field mouse, which made a hasty retreat

Into her hole, there was no living creature in sight.

With loud-beating heart, the learned man took his way into the village. The bells were no longer heard; but, instead, came the merry sounds of fiddles and flutes. A wedding procession was passing through the narrow village street.

The bridegroom, a splendid young peasant, looked happy and proud, — as though he would ask the dear Lord, "How much would you take for the world?" The bride, adorned with a glittering crown, cast her eyes modestly on the ground. Once only she raised her lids; and her eyes, her big black eyes, betrayed to the schoolmaster who it was that was walking under the bridal wreath. And the poor man turned him about and went back, unrecognized, by the way he had come.

It was midday. Green-gold shone the fields; and wherever there was running water, there the sun scattered thousands and thousands of glistening sparkles. The creatures rejoiced in the sunlight; but to-day it was painful to the schoolmaster, and he shaded his eyes with his hand. Thus he strode along.

A traveller joined him, who must have already gone a long distance; for he looked like a wandering cloud of dust.

"Good friend," said the stranger to the school-master, "the sunlight blinds your eyes, does it not?"

The schoolmaster assented.

"See!" continued the other, "there is no better help for it than a pair of gray spectacles such as I wear. Try them once!" And with these words he took the spectacles off his nose, and handed them to the schoolmaster.

The latter consented, and put on the dull-colored glasses. They really did his hot eyes good. The sun lost its bright glare; the meadow, with its red and yellow flowers, the trees and bushes, and the roof of heaven, — everything was gray. And so it seemed quite right to the schoolmaster.

"Are you willing to sell them?" he asked of the strange traveller.

"They are in good hands," was the reply, "and I always carry several pairs of such spectacles with me. Keep them to remember me by, Herr Magister."

"Ah, do you know me? And may I ask — "

"Who I am?" interrupted the stranger, finishing out the question. "My name is Grumbler. Farewell!"

With these words he struck into a bypath, and soon was out of sight. The schoolmaster pressed the gray glasses firmly on his nose, and went his way.

Years had fled since this took place; the schoolmaster had become a crusty old bachelor, and had forgotten how to find pleasure in the world. He still went out into the fields; but the green of the trees and the marvellous coloring of the flowers no longer existed for him. He pulled up the plants by their roots, carried them home, and pressed and dried them; then he laid the flower-mummies on gray blotting-paper, wrote a Latin name beneath: and this was his only pleasure, if pleasure it could be called.

One day, during one of his expeditions, the schoolmaster came to an out-of-the-way valley; through it flowed a brook, which turned a mill; and as he was thirsty, he asked the old woman, who was sunning herself before the door, if she would give him a drink. The old woman said yes, invited the guest to sit down, and went into the house. Soon after, a young girl brought some bread and milk, and placed them on a stone table before the guest. Then the schoolmaster wondered whether the maiden were ugly; but he could not quite make out through his gray spectacles; and he could not take off the spectacles, because he thought the sunlight would hurt his eyes. In silence he ate what was set before him; and as the miller's daughter would take no pay, he pressed her hand and went away. But she looked after the melancholy man till he disappeared behind the bushes.

The meadow valley in which the mill stood must have fostered many kinds of strange plants; for, three days after his first visit, the learned schoolmaster came again and had a talk at the mill. And he came more and more often, and was soon a welcome guest.

He brought sugar, coffee, snuff, and other judicious gifts, to the old grandmother, and entertained the miller with edifying conversation; but to his fair-haired little daughter he said never a word, but contented himself with looking at the beautiful girl, from time to time, through his gray spectacles. Then the miller would nudge the grandmother gently with his elbow, and the old woman would nod her white head.

One day, when the schoolmaster had left the mill and was going along the edge of the meadow, he noticed a mole, caught in a snare, kicking and struggling to escape death on the gallows. The good-hearted man stepped up to him, set the prisoner free, and put him on the ground. Then mole and schoolmaster each went his way.

As the learned man was sitting in his study, on the evening of the same day, it happened that a bat came flying in at the open window. That was not at all strange; but that on the bat rode a little man, no bigger than your finger, and that this little man got down and made a low bow before the schoolmaster, — this, indeed, appeared very extraordinary.

"What do you want here?" he asked the little creature, not very graciously. "Go to some story-teller, and don't disturb the work of sensible people!"

But the little man did not allow himself to be confused. He came nearer, sat down on the box of writing-sand, and said: —

"Do not send me away from you! I have

kind intentions towards you, for you helped me
out of serious trouble to-day; I was the mole
that you released from the snare."

"So! And who are you, in reality?" asked
the scholar, inspecting the little fellow through
his glasses. He had a dainty, trim figure; and
if the spectacles had not been gray, the schoolmaster could have seen that the little man
wore a green coat and a golden-yellow cap.

"I am the meadow sprite, Ranunculus," said
the dwarf. "My servants care for the grass
and the flowers; some wash them with dew,
others comb them with sunbeams, and still
others carry food to the roots. The last-named
I wished to watch at their work this morning,
and, that they might not recognize me, I took
the form of a mole. By this means I fell into
the snare from which your hand set me free.
And now I am here to thank you, and to do
you some service in return."

"What can you mean?" said the schoolmaster.

"You are a learned man," continued Ranunculus. "You are familiar with the flowers and
plants in the meadow and on the mountain, in
the woods and fields; but there is one flower
you do not know."

"What is that?" asked the schoolmaster, excitedly.

"It is the flower called heart's-joy."

"No, I do not know it."

"But I do," said Ranunculus, "and I will tell you where to find it. If you follow along the mill brook, — which you are familiar with, — to its source, you will come to a rock. There you will find a cave, which the people call the goblin's cavern, and, in front of the entrance, blooms the flower heart's-joy, but only on Trinity Sunday, at the hour of sunrise; and whoever is on the spot then can pluck the blossom. Do you understand all that I have said?"

"Perfectly."

"Then good luck to you!" said the little man; and he mounted his winged steed, and flew out at the open window.

The schoolmaster rubbed his forehead, in amazement, and shook his head. Then he buried himself in a folio volume bound in pigskin.

A couple of days after this occurrence, at the hour of twilight, the miller's pretty daughter sat before the meadow mill, and the grandmother by her side. The spinning-wheels hummed; and the old woman was telling the story of Lady Perchta, who sends the swiftest spinners knots of flax which afterwards change to yellow gold, and about other marvels of the sort. She related, too, about the sleeping man who sits in the goblin's cave. Once in a hundred years he becomes visible; and if a maiden kisses him then three times, he is released, and as a reward, the maiden will be given a sweetheart. The old woman went on telling stories; and the pretty maiden listened, and spun the fairy tales further, like the threads of flax which she twisted in her white fingers. The stars rose in the sky; and as it was the time of year when the elder-tree was in bloom, sweet weariness came over the maiden's eyes. She sought her chamber, and went to rest.

In the night she dreamed that there came to her a little man wearing a green coat and a golden-yellow cap. And the little being looked very friendly, and said to the maiden : —

"Thou lucky child! For thee, and none other, the sweetheart in the goblin's cavern is destined. To-morrow is the day when the sleeping man becomes visible. At sunrise he will sit, slumbering, at the entrance of the

cave; and if thou art not afraid, and wilt
kiss him heartily three times on the mouth,
the spell will be broken, and the sweetheart
won. But take great care, while working his
release, not to speak a word, or even to utter
a sound; for, otherwise, the sleeping man will
sink three thousand fathoms deep into the
earth, and will have to wait another hundred
years for his ransom."

Thus spoke the sprite, and vanished. But
the maiden awoke and rubbed her eyes. A
sweet odor, as from new-mown hay, filled the
chamber, and the gray morning light peeped in
through the cracks of the shutters. Then the
damsel, full of courage, arose from her couch,
and dressed herself. Quietly she left the house,
and, tucking up her petticoats, hastened through
the dewy grass to the goblin's cavern.

In the boughs the wood birds were already
stirring, and, still half-asleep, were beginning to
tune up their songs. The white mist sank to
the earth, and spread out in streaks over the
meadow; and the tips of the fir-trees took on
a golden tinge. There stood the miller's lovely
daughter at the entrance of the cavern; and
truly, just as the little drawf had predicted,

there sat the sleeping man on a moss-covered stone. The maiden almost uttered a loud cry; for the sleeping man looked so exactly like the schoolmaster, even to wearing a pair of gray glasses on his nose.

Fortunately the damsel bethought herself of the little man's warning; and silently, but with a loud-beating heart, she drew near the sleeper to perform the benignant task of setting him free — and it did not seem to her nearly as frightful as she had imagined beforehand.

Gently she bent over the slumberer, and kissed him on the mouth; the man stirred, as if he would awaken.

The maiden kissed him a second time; the man opened his weary eyelids, and looked at the damsel dreamily through his gray spectacles.

But she remained resolute, and pressed the third kiss on his lips.

Then the man, fully awake, jumped up from his seat in such haste that the glasses fell from his nose and broke into a thousand pieces on the stony ground. And he saw again, for the first time in many years, the verdure of spring gleaming in the sunlight, the bright flowers, the blue sky, and, in the midst of all this glory,

a maiden as beautiful as a May rose and slender as a lily.   And he took her in his arms,
and gave her the three kisses back again, and
countless others followed these.

But on a bright yellow marigold sat the
meadow sprite Ranunculus, kicking his little
legs for joy.   Then he jumped down, making
the flower shake violently, and went about his
momentous affairs.   He had kept his word:
the schoolmaster had found his heart's-joy, and
the miller's pretty daughter her sweetheart.

THE LEGEND OF THE DAISY.

GOOD children, as you know, when they die,
go to heaven and become angels. But if
you have the least idea that there they do nothing
the livelong day but fly about and play hide and
seek behind the clouds, you are very much mistaken.

Angel children, like the boys and girls upon
earth, are obliged to go to school, and on week-
days they have to sit three hours in the morning
and two in the afternoon in the angel school.
There they write with golden pencils on silver
slates, and instead of A-B-C-books they have
books of fairy tales with colored pictures. They
do not study geography, for why should they in
heaven learn about the earth? and they know
nothing about the multiplication table in eternity.
The teacher of the angel school is Dr. Faust.
He was a professor on earth; and on account of
a certain story, which cannot be repeated here,

he has to keep school three thousand years longer
in heaven before the long vacation begins for him.
The little angels have Wednesday and Saturday
afternoons for a half-holiday; then Dr. Faust
takes them to play on the Milky Way. But
Sundays they are allowed to play in the great
meadow in front of the Heavenly Gate, and they
look forward to this all through the week. The
meadow is not green, but blue, and there grow
thousands and thousands of silver and golden
flowers. They shine in the night, and we people
on earth call them stars. When the angels gam-
bol before the Heavenly Gate, Dr. Faust is not
with them, for he has so much trouble during
the week that he must rest on Sunday. Then
the holy Peter, who guards the Gate of Heaven,
takes the oversight of them. He sees that they
are very orderly in their play, and that none of
them runs or flies away; but if it happen that
one gets too far from the gate, then he whistles
with his golden key: that means "Come back!"

Once, it was so very hot in heaven that Saint
Peter fell asleep. As soon as the angels noticed
it, they swarmed out hither and thither and were
scattered over the whole meadow. The most
enterprising started on a voyage of discovery, and

finally came to the place where the world is shut off by a high fence. At first they sought for a crack somewhere to peep through; but when they found there was not a chink, they climbed and flew up on the fence and looked over.

Over there on the other side was Hades, and before the gate of Hades was just such another throng of little imps roving about. They were black as coals, and had horns on their heads and long tails behind. One of them by accident looked up and saw the angels, and immediately besought them eagerly to let them into heaven for a little while: — they would be very proper and well-behaved.

This touched the angels; and as the little black fellows pleased them, they decided that they might grant the poor imps this innocent pleasure. One of them knew where Jacob's ladder was kept. They dragged it out of the lumber-room (Saint Peter was fortunately still asleep), lifted it over the fence, and let it down into Hades. The long-tailed imps climbed up the rounds like monkeys, the angels gave them their hands, and so the little scapegraces came into the heavenly meadow.

At first they behaved themselves very well. They went about properly, carrying their tails

like trains in their arms, just as Satan's grandmother, who lays great stress upon good manners,
had taught them. But it did not last long; they
became lawless, turned summersaults and hand-
springs, and screamed like veritable devil-urchins.
They teased the beautiful moon, who was looking
peacefully out of one of the heavenly windows;
they ran out their tongues and made long noses
at her, and finally they began to pull up the
flowers growing in the meadow and to throw
them down on the earth.

Now the angels were sorry and repented bitterly of having let unclean guests into heaven.
They besought and threatened; but the imps
would not stop, and grew wilder and wilder.

Then the angels, in their anxiety, wakened
Saint Peter, and confessed penitently what they
had done. He threw his hands together over his
head, when he became aware of the mischief that
was going on. "March in!" he thundered; and
the little ones stole back with drooping wings
through the gate into heaven. Then Saint Peter
called a couple of strong angels to him. They
caught the little imps up together and carried
them back where they belonged.

The little angels did not escape punishment.

For three Sundays, one after another, they could not go to the Heavenly Gate; and when they went out to walk, they had to take off their wings and lay aside their halos, and it is a great disgrace for an angel to have to go without wings and halo.

But some good came of the affair, after all. The flowers which the imps tore up and threw down on the earth took root and multiplied year after year. To be sure, the star-flowers lost much of their heavenly beauty, but they are still lovely to see, with their golden-yellow disks and crown of silver-white rays. And because they are of heavenly origin they possess a wonderful virtue. If a maid with doubt in her heart pulls off the white petals of the starry blossom one by one, and at the same time repeats a certain saying, she will know very truly by the last leaflet what she longs to find out.

THE CLOVER LEAF.

THE town was as silent as the grave, for all who
were not compelled by sickness or infirmity
to stay at home had gone out to the park, where
the shooting-club were trying to shoot down, piece
by piece, from the pole the two-headed eagle, the
emblem of the holy Roman Empire. In the cot-
tages, decked with wreaths of evergreen and
trimmed with bright-colored banners, sat the
townspeople drinking beer and foaming ale. Red-
cheeked maidens with white aprons and bare arms
stood behind the sausage ovens, fanning away the
smoke rising from the coals. All kinds of itiner-
ant people dressed in gay-colored tatters were prac-
tising their arts here, — knife-throwers, fire-eaters,
and acrobats with hoarse voices, vaunting their
skill, and a bear was performing his clumsy dance
to the sound of a Polish bagpipe.

From the club-house, out of whose gable windows
fluttered the banners which the Emperor Henry

had presented to the club, sounded the ceaseless
cracking of the heavy arquebuses, and the eagle on
the pole had already lost his sceptre and imperial
ball, as well as a claw and a wing. The men who
on week-days wielded hammer and plane, axe and
awl, managed the firearms as skilfully as the tools
of their handicraft, and looked very magnificent in
their shooting-jackets. But while shooting they
did not forget to drink, and the great bumper,
which was decorated with wild beasts in embossed
work, circulated freely.

Among the women who were present at the club-
house watching the skill of the men, was a slender
young maiden not less conspicuous for her beauty
than for her costume. She was dressed in the
usual style of the country people; but her dark
gown was of fine Brabant cloth, the buttons on her
waist were of solid silver, and her black silk cap,
from beneath which hung down her long yellow
braids, had a gold ornament, which would have
been cheap at two crowns. The city damsels
noticed with displeasure how the young fellows
assiduously crowded about the table where the
maiden sat, and turned up their little noses at the
country mouse and the want of taste in the young
men. However, it contributed somewhat to their

peace of mind that all the endeavors of the city
young men to get next the maiden were in vain.
She was sitting between the king's forester, a
man of sunburnt face and iron-gray beard, and
a wild-looking huntsman's lad. The neighboring
seats were also occupied, and, indeed, with none
but huntsmen, so the beautiful girl might be considered well protected. The old man next her was
her father, but the young hunter on the other side
of her was her father's assistant. He had made
the best shots of the day, and the city fellows envied
him no less his good luck in the match than his
seat next the beautiful Margaret. But she did not
seem to be greatly edified by the nearness of the
young fellow; she answered his questions in mono-
syllables only, and when he attempted to sit nearer,
she gathered the folds of her dress together as
though she were afraid of being touched by the
wild youth.

Now the voice of the herald sounded through
the enclosure: "Forester Henner, make ready!"
The maiden's father rose from his seat, to take his
turn in shooting at the bird, and the young hunter
followed at the old man's heels.

Already there was nothing left of the noble
eagle but his tail. But whoever should shoot this

down from the pole would be king of the tournament.

The forester took aim, and shot. The people
saw how the tail trembled and bent forward, but
it did not fall to the ground. The cry of joy which
some had already raised, ceased suddenly, and the
forester planted his gunstock angrily on the ground.

Now came Witsch's turn, for such was the young
hunter's name. He raised his gun and moved his
lips in a whisper. Then happened something very
extraordinary. The eagle's tail, as though it afterwards thought better of it, detached itself from
the pole and fell to the ground, like an over-ripe
apple from a tree. The hunter's gun went off too
late; the bullet whistled through empty air.

Malicious laughter arose, and everybody was
pleased at the young fellow's bad luck, for the
sunburned Witsch was one whom nobody had
confidence in nor wished well. But he did not
seem to take the accident much to heart; indeed,
his voice was the first to salute old Henner
as king of the tournament. The forester's face
beamed with joy, as the chain with the medal was
hung around his neck, and he was proclaimed
king. He bowed his thanks on all sides like a
veritable king, and then they took him into their

midst and showed him to the crowd. The drum-
mers and buglers marched ahead, and then came
the color-bearer, who, according to an ancient custom, went dancing along with wonderful agility.
These were followed by the king of the festival,
accompanied by the heralds ; behind him marched
the prize-winners, and foremost among them was
Witsch; then the scorers, with the pieces of the
shattered bird; and last of all the other members
of the club. The procession moved in a circle
around the park, and then turned back into the
club-house, where the king's supper was to end the
festival.

As soon as they reached there, the king of the
tournament went up to his assistant, seized him
by the hand, and said distinctly and loud enough
to be heard by everybody: " Witsch, I am both
glad and sorry for what has happened. This
honor has escaped you, but you are still the
better marksman of us two. Yes, dear friends,"
and he turned to the others, "there is not one
among you who can outdo him."

There was a murmur of dissatisfaction in the
circle of the marksmen. Then the brown country
youth cast his eyes over the assembled crowd and
screwed up his mouth. He looked up where, high

in the air, the chimney swallows were darting
hither and thither.

"Who among you," he asked, "will venture to
bring down two swallows with one bullet?"

The huntsmen were silent.

But Witsch raised his gun, took aim for a moment, fired, and two mangled swallows fell to the
ground.

"Did you see that?" called out the old Henner.
"No, nobody can equal that."

The men were silent, and many looked askance
at the uncanny huntsman, who stood there, as
though the shot were an every-day occurrence. But
the forester took him by the arm, led him to the
table, and bade him sit by his daughter.

Those who had not the privilege to drink at the
club table did so in a cottage in the park; and at
the little tables, highly decorated with wet circles,
the master-shot of the huntsman Witsch was dis-
cussed on all sides.

"Did you hear what he whispered before he
shot at the tail on the pole?" asked the herald, who
was resting from his work behind the tankard.

"'Skill brings not
The lucky shot.'

That is how the saying ran. I stood near by. I

heard it. That is a benediction he didn't learn
in church. It would have been an easy thing for
him to shoot down the bird himself and become
king of the festival, but the sly fox lets the old
man have the honor and wins the daughter."

"And what do you think of the shot at the
swallows?" one of the scorers asked the herald.

The old man shook his gray head. He had been
a soldier, and knew a thing or two about such mat-
ters. He began to tell about charmed bullets, en-
chantments, and the fernseed which makes things
invisible. He also told dreadful stories of the
Wild Huntsman, who rides through the clouds at
night, and all kinds of ghost stories, so that his
listeners became more and more excited.

A tempest was gathering over the head of the
young hunter Witsch. The sorcerer, the magic
shooter, ought to be tried for his life, thought a
troubled master-tailor. But the others were more
inclined to the opinion of a boisterous journeyman-
smith, who proposed to brand Witsch on the back,
so that he might remember the tournament all the
rest of his life.

Night was falling; the club-house became empty.
But the old Henner still sat drinking with his com-
rades, and paid no attention to his daughter, who
repeatedly pulled at his jacket to remind him that it

was time to go.   One can more easily entice a fox
from his hole than a forester from his beer.

Hunting and shooting adventures were here, too,
the subjects of conversation, and the most incredi-
ble stories were served up in the most classic huntsman's slang.   But not the least wonderful was the
little anecdote of the three marksmen and the
clover leaf.   The story ran thus : —

Three wandering hunters once stopped at a
forest tavern and disposed themselves comfortably.
As soon as they had partaken abundantly of food
and drink, they called the host to them and asked
him if he would like to see something, the like of
which nobody had ever seen before.   This gratified
the host, and he offered them free drinks.   Then
one of them picked a clover leaf, the second
brought a ladder and fastened the clover leaf to
the gable of the house, while the third measured
off a hundred paces and called his companions to
follow.   Then the first one began and shot off the
first leaf, the second hit the second, and the third
the third.   The host was amazed, and gave each
of the fellows another drink and was glad when
they went away.

"If that is true," said old Henner, "the fellows shot with charmed bullets."

And so thought the others.

The sunburned Witsch, however, only laughed and said it was child's play; he would agree to do the same thing.

"But if somebody else should load the gun?" asked one of the men, distrustfully.

"Whoever will may load the gun," boldly replied Witsch; "but he must be honest about it."

"If you are successful," exclaimed the old Henner, half intoxicated, "then, young man, I will give you whatever you may ask of me, as a prize."

"Father!" admonished the maiden, in dismay.

"Whatever you may ask of me," repeated the forester.

"Well, then," said Witsch slowly, "I will shoot the little leaves of a clover from the stem, a hundred paces off, with three bullets and three shots, and you promise to give me as a prize whatever I may ask of you. Is it a bargain?"

"Don't do it, father! don't do it!" cried the maiden, in genuine terror.

"Thou little fool!" said the father, laughing; and the woodsmen joined in the laughter. No one had the least doubt what the hunter would demand as his reward, and they took poor Margaret's anguish for a maiden's modesty.

"It is a bargain!" cried the forester, reaching
out his hand, "my word —"

"Wait!" interrupted an old huntsman. "Sup-
posing the little affair is not successful, what shall
the shooter pay as a forfeit?"

"Whatever you say," answered Witsch.

Margaret had risen from her seat; she was as
pale as death.

"Then he shall go," she said, "as far as his feet
can carry him, and never come into my sight
again."

Witsch bit his lips.

"All right, miss," said he, gritting his teeth;
"so shall it be. Your hand, forester! I give you
my word of honor."

The agreement was sealed.

While the old man was reprimanding his
daughter in a trembling voice, the sunburned
Witsch took a hasty departure and went on his
way. Outside the club-house a crowd of sturdy,
boisterous fellows were hiding, but the one for
whom they lay in wait escaped them. He probably carried fernseed with him.

* * *

In a clearing of the wood at the foot of the
Thorstein mountain lay the keeper's lodge, where

old Henner dwelt. Sad at heart, he sat before the door on the stone seat, and the spotted blood-hound who was lying down not far away looked up from time to time at his master. He would have gladly expressed his sympathy by a dumb caress, but he thought it wiser not to come too near the ill-humored man. The old man was displeased with himself, but still he would not admit it. He would have given his little finger if he could have taken back the agreement he had made with his assistant, for it was clear to him now that his child had an unconquerable aversion to Witsch, and although he tried to console himself with the thought that dislike is often changed to affection in the marriage state, still, in the bottom of his heart he wished that Witsch might not succeed in the clover trial.

On Midsummer day, which, according to an old custom, is kept as a holiday by the huntsmen, the forester's assistant was to prove his skill, and Midsummer day was not far distant. The poor little Margaret went about pale as the wood-nymph who sometimes meets the shepherds and charcoal-burners on moonlight nights, and the father hardly had the heart to look into her eyes, red with weeping.

Now Margaret had a goat named Whitecoat, and in all the mountains round there was no goat that could equal her in intelligence. Whitecoat saw very clearly that her mistress was troubled in heart, and when she was led to the meadow, she no longer leaped gayly about Margaret as was her wont, but went sadly along behind her with drooping ears.

Midsummer eve had come. The keeper's lodge was trimmed with wreaths of evergreen and garlands of leaves for the reception of the guests; but the inmates went about as though there had been a death in the house.

Margaret had milked her goat, and now was sitting on the milking-stool, with her hands folded in her lap, and weeping bitterly.

"Oh, Whitecoat," she said sorrowfully, "why should I be so wretched?"

It seemed as though the goat had only been waiting for her to speak to her, for to the maiden's astonishment she opened her rosy mouth and said: —

"Thou speakest at a propitious hour. In the sacred Midsummer night, when everything is set free and transformed, we animals have the power of speech, and I may answer thee. Tell me what

troubles thee, and perhaps I can help thee: I am
no ordinary goat."

"What are you, then?" asked the damsel.
"Are you perhaps an enchanted princess?"

"No," answered Whitecoat; "I am something
better than that. I am descended in a direct
line from one of the goats who in ancient times
used to draw the carriage of the old man who
sleeps yonder in the Thornstein. But thou knowest nothing about that. However, believe me,
I am more than other, ordinary goats, and I am
willing to help thee, if it is in my power."

"Oh, good Whitecoat, if you only could!"

And so Margaret related her trouble.

The goat listened attentively. When the
maiden had finished, she said: —

"Thou must never belong to the sunburnt
Witsch. He is in league with the devil, and I
know why. To-morrow it will be three years
since I watched him in the forest. It was about
the hour of noon, over on yonder meadow. There
he stood and spread out a white cloth before him,
and just as the sun's disk reached the zenith, he
shot at it and three drops of blood fell on the
cloth. He took it up and hid it in his bosom.
Since that time he has never missed a shot, and

to-morrow he will hit the little clover leaves, too, even if he stand a hundred miles away from the mark."

"You see, it is impossible to help me," said Margaret, with a groan.

"Perhaps not," returned Whitecoat. "It would not be the first time that sorcery has come to nought. Lead me to-morrow before sunrise to the meadow, and perhaps I may find a way to help you."

"Where is the girl hiding?" at this moment called out the scolding voice of old Henner, putting his head through the window of the stable. "Gone to sleep while milking! — Come out, Margaret, and get my supper ready."

The maiden jumped up from the milking-stool, where she had fallen asleep, stroked good White-coat's head, and went to her father.

The dream — for such it must have been — kept going round and round in the maiden's head. Before daybreak she led the goat to the meadow, and when she brought her back later to the lodge, Whitecoat sprang gayly along like a young kid, and Margaret looked peaceful, or rather almost happy, so that her father shook his gray head in surprise.

The invited guests came, and among them was the forester's assistant Witsch. He looked about insolently and seemed sure of his success. Margaret welcomed him just the same as she did the other guests, but she avoided him as much as possible.

When the guests were all present, old Henner stepped into their circle and renewed the promise which he had given to his assistant at the tournament, and the latter announced that he was ready at a moment's notice to prove his skill.

The forester looked anxiously at his daughter and said : —

"Get a clover leaf at once, and fasten it with wax to the barn door."

A clover leaf was already at hand, and Margaret fastened it to the door with trembling fingers.

The young hunter measured his distance. A hundred paces had been stipulated, but the arrogant fellow doubled the number of his own free will. The clover leaf could hardly be seen from this great distance. One of the huntsmen loaded the gun before the eyes of the others and handed it to the marksman. He raised the gun and fired, apparently without taking aim; he let the other two shots follow just as quickly.

"Now go and see!" he cried, sure of his success, and looked with wild joy towards the beautiful Margaret, who stood in the distance, with quick-beating heart.

The witnesses hastened to the barn door, while Witsch went towards the maiden.

Then they called out to him : —

"Witsch, you have lost; one little leaf still remains on the stem."

"Impossible!" cried the huntsman, rushing towards the door. But it was no illusion. The three bullets had pierced the wood one after another, but on the stem of the clover still hung one uninjured leaf.

The huntsman's black eyes shot fire. Then he raised his fist towards heaven and uttered such a horrible curse that it made the cold shivers run down the men's backs, and then without a word he strode off into the wild forest.

But the beautiful Margaret had hastened to her goat, and laughing and weeping embraced the neck of her rescuer.

The wise Whitecoat had led the maiden that morning to a place where she found a four-leaved clover, and no magic could make a marksman hit four leaflets with three shots.

The uncanny Witsch never let himself be seen again in the neighborhood; it was as if the earth had swallowed him up. Afterward, the forest people say they have seen him in the company of the wild huntsman, but the matter remains quite uncertain.

The marks of the three bullets can still be seen in the barn door, and a descendant of the wise goat Whitecoat was shown to me when I heard the wonderful tale related on the spot, and so the story must indeed be true.

THE ADDER-QUEEN.

THERE was once a young shepherd who possessed two things besides the homely clothes
which he wore on his back, — his fife, and his
Mechthild, a plump, brown little maid with lips
as red as cherries. The fife he had carved out
himself; the maid he had found in the forest,
where her father burned charcoal. They were
both agreed that some time they would become
man and wife. The old charcoal-burner had nothing against it either, and they might have been
married right away if they had had anything
besides their love; but love alone, be it ever so
warm, will not cook the supper nor heat the
children's broth. "So, let us wait," thought
they, and hoped for better times. One day the
beautiful Mechthild was sitting not far from the
charcoal kiln, where her father was busy stirring
the fire, and near her stood her lover, while the
sheep were wandering about in the wood, guarded

by the dog. Over the maiden's head an old mountain-ash spread its boughs, from which hung bunches of scarlet berries. She had plucked a number of them, and was now engaged in string-ing the single berries on a long thread. This made a splendid coral necklace. Wendelin, as the young shepherd was called, watched the maid as she moved her little fingers busily, and then he looked on her rosy cheeks, her smooth brow and all her charms one after another, and thought to himself, "How lovely she is!"

Now the string of jewels was finished. Mech-thild twined it around the tightly twisted braids of her dark-brown hair, and smiled at her lover like a happy child. But he looked suddenly sor-rowful. "Ah, Mechthild," he sighed, "why am I so poor? Why can I not place a gold ring on thy finger or put a garnet necklace around thy neck?"

"It is no worse now than it has been," said the maid, consolingly. "But are the red berries not beautiful?"

The shepherd did not seem to have heard her words. He was looking at the smoke which arose from the charcoal kiln and floated away in blue clouds over the tops of the fir-trees. "Why will good luck never visit me?" said he sadly. "There are so many treasures lying concealed and be-witched in the mountains; but fortune only laughs at stupid people; and when they are about to seize the gold exultingly, it sinks miles deep into the earth. I have been into the forest at every hour of the night, but no blue flames light up for me, no pale lady beckons to me, and no dwarf leads me to the treasure in the hollow stone."

"Wendelin," said the maiden, earnestly, "don't go about digging and searching for magic treas-ures! No good will come of it." And she con-tinued playfully, "You can more easily win great riches through the golden-horned stag, on which Lady Holle rides through the forest. Every year the magic deer sheds his antlers. Seek for them, my Wendelin! Those of this year must still be lying somewhere in the wood."

The charcoal-burner had come along and heard the last words. "Oho," he said, "so you would like to find the golden antlers? You ask for a great deal. Wouldn't a handful of golden flax-seed husks do as well? Or how would you like the little crown belonging to the Adder-Queen, who lives under the red stone by the water? If there is anything I wish for, it is the fernseed,

which makes one invisible. Oh, what fun I
would have! What a face the big landlord of
the *Bear* would make up, if every evening I
could make his best beer-barrel lighter and fish
the biggest sausage out of the kettle without his
seeing me!"

They went on talking in the same strain.
Much was said about the magic pervading the
forest, and the shepherd became more and more
thoughtful. He usually played a tune on his
fife to his sweetheart before he left her; but to-
day he never gave it a thought when the time
came for his departure. With head bent down
he went after the flock, which the dog kept together by his barking.

The sun had almost finished his course, and
a ruddy glow lay on the mountains when the
shepherd came out of the woods with the sheep.
Before him lay a green field, through the midst
of which ran a broad, shallow brook, and on the
further side of the water, like a gigantic grave-
stone, stood a single rock of a reddish color.
Bramble-bushes and golden-yellow broom grew
luxuriantly about it, and to the crevices clung
moss and wild thyme. Here, then. was where the
Adder-Princess was said to dwell.

After the sheep had satisfied their thirst, the
shepherd drove them through the brook, for the
town where he and the flock belonged lay on the
other side of the mountain. He intended to pass
by the red stone as usual, but he stood chained
to the spot, for it seemed to him as if something
stirred in the bushes.

"If it should be the Adder-Queen!" thought
he; and as he had once heard that snakes loved
to hear violin and flute playing, he drew his fife
out of his shepherd's pouch, and began to play a
gentle melody.

But lo and behold! There, out of the broom,
arose the head of a great white snake, forking
her tongue and wearing a shining crown.

The youth was so frightened that he stopped
playing his fife, and in a twinkling the Adder
had vanished.

What the charcoal-burner had said was true
then. The shepherd timidly retreated, and drove
the flock in a wide circuit around the stone to
the town.

The Adder-Queen, or, rather, her golden crown,
lay on his mind day and night. But how should
he contrive to get possession of the ornament?
The old village blacksmith was a wise man, and

knew a great deal besides how to eat his bread; perhaps something might be learned about it from him. So he betook himself one evening to the blacksmith's, after the master and his apprentices had left off working; for a pretence, asked some advice in regard to a sick sheep, and after beating about the bush for some time, finally brought the conversation round to the Adder-Queen. He had come to the right person. The old blacksmith knew quite enough about the ways to get possession of the little crown, and was not at all loth to show his knowledge.

"Whoever would rob the Adder-Queen of her crown," he explained, " has nothing more to do than to spread a white cloth on the ground before the hole where she lives. Immediately the snake will come out, lay the jewel on the cloth, and disappear again. Now is the time to seize it quickly, and with all possible speed to strive to reach water. For as soon as the Adder-Queen notices that she has been robbed, she will start after the fugitive, hissing frightfully; and if he cannot get across water, he is a dead man. But if he is fortunate enough to reach the farther shore, the serpent can do him no harm, and the crown is his."

This was the blacksmith's story, and the shep‑
herd drank in every word.

Some days later the beautiful daughter of the
charcoal-burner was sitting in front of their cottage. All of a sudden her lover came running
with all his might, threw a little sparkling coro-
net into her lap, and dropped lifeless on the
ground.

Mechthild gave a scream. Her father came to
her, and a glance at the jewel told him what
had happened. "He has stolen the little crown
from the Adder-Queen," said he. Then he lifted
the swooning youth, bore him into the hut, and
tried to bring him back to consciousness.

His efforts were successful, but the whole night
long he lay tossing in delirium on the couch of
leaves: not till morning did rest come to him.

In the course of the day he recovered entirely
and was able to talk. Anxiety and care retreated
from the charcoal-burner's cottage, and joy entered in. There lay the hard-won serpent's jewel
before the lovers, who sat together hand in hand,
making plans for the future. Of course they
could not keep the little crown; it must go to
the goldsmith's in the town: but in its place the
bridal wreath would soon adorn the beautiful

Mechthild's head; and after the wedding festiv-
ities were over, Wendelin would take his young
wife to a pleasant little house, and they would
kindle a fire on their own hearth. Oh, blissful
time! Oh, blissful time!

On the following morning Wendelin returned
to the village. He wisely avoided the red stone.

The Adder-Queen's crown had twelve points,
each tipped with a blood-red stone. As soon
as her lover was gone, Mechthild took it out of
the chest, where she had hidden it away, and
placed it on her head. It was indeed a very
different ornament from the red berries of the
mountain-ash. If she only could see how becoming the jewels were; but there was no looking-
glass in the charcoal-burner's cottage. Whenever
Mechthild wished to look at her nut-brown face,
she ran to the well-spring, which bubbled up out
of the mould of the forest, not far from the char-
coal-kiln; and hither she turned her footsteps
now. She bent over the clear water, and was
charmed with her sparkling ornament. "You
like me, don't you?" she said to a fat frog sitting on the edge of the spring. And the frog
said, "Gloog!" jumped into the water, and dived
under to tell the lady-frog at the bottom what

a wonderful sight he had beheld. A gray-green
lizard rustled through the leaves; she raised her
head and looked curiously at the bejewelled
maid. Then she slipped away into her underground chamber, and told her sisters about the
beautiful damsel with the crown in her hair.
And the blue titmice came fluttering inquisi-
tively by, and the golden-crested wrens bristled
their tufts with envy, when they saw the glistening jewels on the maiden's head. The squirrel peeped out curiously from behind the trunk
of a pine-tree, and a weasel frisked about over
the wood-plants to take a look at the crowned
maiden.

Tramp, tramp, now sounded in her ears; perhaps it was a red deer, attracted by the glitter
of her crown. But no; stags and does do not
tread the earth with hoofs that are shod: it is
the sound of horses. Bright dresses could be
seen between the branches of the trees, and the
merry sound of people's voices came through
the air. She sprang away from the brim of the
well, and was about to hasten to the house,
but the riders had already drawn up in front of
the charcoal-burner's cottage. There were gentlemen in rich hunting-costume and ladies in

long, flowing riding-dresses, slender young falcon-
ers, and sunburned huntsmen with long beards.

The maiden dropped a low courtesy. The
stately gentleman on the roan horse was the
count who owned the land, and the beautiful
lady by his side was his young wife.

Mechthild replied respectfully to the question
concerning the nearest way to the meadow,
through which the water flowed. Then the
countess caught sight of the crown on the maid-
en's head, and cried out in the greatest surprise,
"Tell me, my dear girl, how you came by such
jewelry as that."

The maiden, in her embarrassment, made no
reply; but the charcoal-burner, who had come
along in the meantime, answered shrewdly, "It
is an old heir-loom, most gracious lady; something my great-grandfather brought home from
the war in Italy. If it pleases you, pray take
it."

The countess had the crown brought to her,
and the maids of honor, who accompanied her,
looked curiously at the precious ornament.

"I must have the little crown," said the lady,
casting a tender glance toward the count.

He smiled and unfastened a heavy purse from

his belt. "Take that for the crown," said he to the charcoal-burner; "it is gold. You foolish people have probably never known what a treasure your cottage concealed."

The maids of honor fastened the crown with two silver pins to their lady's velvet hood; then the riders spurred on their horses, waved a farewell to the charcoal-burner and his daughter, and galloped off through the woods.

The hunters had soon left the forest behind, and before them lay the broad meadow valley and the red stone.

The lazily-flowing brook formed here and there pools and little eddies, much frequented by ducks, herons, and other water-fowl. The hawkers gave the falcons over to the ladies, and all eyes were directed towards the reeds surrounding the water.

And now up flew a silver heron, noisily flapping his wings. The countess quickly took the hood from the falcon's head, and let him loose. Screaming, the falcon flew aloft, till he hovered over the heron. Then he swooped down, cleverly avoided the threatening bill, and seized the bird with his talons. For some time there was a fierce struggle in the air; then both circled round and round, and the vanquished heron fell with flapping wings on the meadow near the red stone.

The countess was the first to reach the spot where he fell. Her cheeks glowing with excitement, she sprang out of the saddle to release the heron from the falcon's talons, and to place the silver ring, which bore her name, on his foot. Then she gave a sudden cry and fell on the ground.

Her terrified companions hastened to her side. The count took his young wife in his arms, and anxiously inquired what had happened. She cried out with pain and pointed to her foot. The count bent down, and saw that her silk stocking was stained with a drop of blood.

"You have scratched yourself with a thorn," he said, laughing; "that is nothing." But the lady moaned slightly, her temples began to beat violently, and her face grew as pale as death.

The terror-stricken count gave orders for two huntsmen to go for doctors. He himself wrapped his wife in his mantle, took her in front of him on his saddle, and, followed by the others, galloped at full speed toward the nearest village. There he had a couch prepared for the sufferer, and anxiously waited for the doctors to come.

Her malady grew worse from hour to hour. The old smith, whose advice was asked, looked at the wound and shook his head, and said that it was no thorn-prick, but rather the bite of a poisonous serpent. The same opinion was given later by the doctors. They spoke Latin together, shrugged their shoulders, and used salves and potions as their art prescribed. But they did no good. The sufferer grew weaker and weaker, and when the evening star hung over the forest, she lay unconscious on her bed of pain. Death stood without before the door.

In the meantime Wendelin, the shepherd, was driving his flock home to the village. Mechthild had told him how the countess had purchased the serpent's crown, and then they counted the pieces of gold and took counsel about the spending of the money. Now the shepherd was cheerfully wending his way along in front of his flock and playing a little tune on his fife.

Then suddenly his breath failed him, and his hair stood on end. Out of the bushes before him came the Adder-Queen, and raised her crownless head, forking her tongue at him.

" Stand still, or you shall die ! " hissed the snake. And the poor youth stood still, and clung to his crook with trembling hands.

" Listen, young man, to what I tell you," said the serpent. " The lady who wore my crown is sick unto death; I stung her in the foot. But I guard the plant whose juice will make her well. Follow me, and I will show you the healing herb."

The snake glided through the grass, and the shepherd followed her with beating heart. The adder stopped near the red stone. She broke off an herb and handed it to the shepherd. It was a delicate little plant, and resembled the forked tongue of a serpent.

"Now hasten," said the adder, "as fast as you can to the village where the sick lady lies; and if you let one drop of the sap of the plant fall on her wound, she will be cured. But as a reward demand the crown, and bring it back to me. Swear that you will."

The trembling shepherd swore as the Adder-Queen desired, then hastened to the village, and asked to be taken to the sufferer.

The countess was still living, but her breathing was faint. On her right sat the count, with his face buried in his hands; on her left sat a priest murmuring prayers.

"Try your skill," said the count to the shepherd. "If you succeed in healing her, I will make you rich."

Then the shepherd raised his eyes to Heaven in

a hasty prayer and let one drop of the sap of the herb fall on the wound. The sufferer at once opened her eyes and took a long breath. Then she lifted her beautiful head from the pillows and looked confidingly at her husband. And from that hour the fever left her, and with the dawn the countess' cheeks again took on their rosy color, and all her suffering had passed away.

She gave the crown gladly to the shepherd who had healed her, and he, true to his oath, carried it without delay to the red stone by the water, where the Adder-Queen received it.

The count kept his word too. He presented the shepherd with a stately mansion, in which Mechthild soon made her entrance as bride.

Whether the Adder-Queen still dwells under the red stone by the water, and whether she still wears her little crown, that I cannot tell. But the manor which the count gave to the shepherd, is still standing, and is called *Schlangenhof,* or the Serpent's Court.

THE BLACKSMITH'S BRIDE.

IN the midst of the forest was a black-green lake surrounded by very ancient giant fir-trees. The brooklets which came leaping down from every height like wanton kids, grew more and more quiet as they approached the pond, and finally flowed silently into the dark water. And when they came into sight again at the outlet of the lake, united in a stately stream, it was as if they had seen something uncanny, for they ran swiftly over gravel and stones, and only when they had left a good bit of their course behind them, did the waters again begin to murmur and to babble, and the white-breasted water-thrush, whose nest was on the bank, overheard strange things.

Now there lived in one of the villages which lay scattered among the forest mountains a young fisherman who earned his livelihood with net and hook. The bright-colored trout in the brooks crowded about the bait that he threw to them, and

when he drew his net through the waters of the
forest lake, huge pike and big bream with long
whiskers floundered in the meshes, so that he had
some difficulty in bringing his haul to land.

One day he was sitting on the shore of the lake
watching his hook. It seemed to him that just
beneath the smooth surface he saw a woman's face
of rare beauty. He was frightened, and jumped
up from his seat. Just then there was a rustling
in the bushes, and when he turned around he
looked into the mild eyes of a maiden carrying
a scythe over her shoulders.

"Are you busy, Heini?" asked the pretty
maid; and the fisherman told her what he was
doing.

" Heini," continued the maiden, "let me give
you some advice; it is kindly meant. Let the fish
be in the lake. The people tell dreadful stories
about — about — "

" About the water-sprite," interrupted the
youth.

" Be still! for Heaven's sake, be still!" said the
maiden, timidly. " Listen to me, Heini, and keep
away from these quiet waters. You will find fish
enough somewhere else. It would be a pity if you
should some day find your cottage afloat on the
water."

"Gertrude," said the fisherman, angrily, "why must you worry so about that?"

The maiden turned aside. "Yes, I should feel badly, very badly, for I love you like a sister. You have known that for a long time."

"Like a sister," sighed the youth, and then they were silent.

A fish leaped up out of the water, and Heini seized his rod as if in a dream.

"Good by," said the maiden.

"Good by, Gertrude. Where are you going?"

"To the blacksmith's. The scythe — You know it is haying-time now. The blacksmith has to mend the scythe."

"Go, then!" said the fisherman, roughly, and turned his face towards the lake.

Once more the maiden called out in a gentle voice, "Good by, Heini; do as I have asked you."

But the youth gave her no answer. The maiden turned away, and went on into the woods.

Silent and sullen, the fisherman looked after his jerking rod, and as he cut open the throat of a big pike that he had caught, his eyes shone with an uncanny light.

The young fellow sat a long time by the pond.

The mountain-tops took on a rosy hue, and the trees cast long shadows on the mirror-like surface of the water. A magpie fluttered along, laughed in her way, and said : —

> " ' Black and white is the suit I wear;
> Black the smith, but the maiden fair.
> When the smith his love embraced,
> Her lily-white brow with soot was defaced."

With a loud laugh the magpie flew off into the dark forest, and the fisherman hastily gathered up his belongings and left the lake with a heavy heart.

* * *

Weeks and weeks had passed away. Heini was again sitting by the pond in the forest, but he was not fishing. He was leaning his head on his hands and gazing into the water. The poor fellow looked utterly wretched; the color had faded from his cheeks, and his eyes were dull and sad. And as he thus gazed down into the depths of the water, he thought that he again saw the form of a lovely woman, beckoning to him with her white hand.

"Yes, it would be much better for me if I were laid away down below there," he groaned. "Oh, if it were only all ended!"

A low chuckling startled him. He looked around; but this time it was no rosy-cheeked maiden, but an old, toothless woman, who stood behind him. On her arm hung a basket full of scarlet toad-stools.

"Oh, it is you, is it, Mother Bridget?"

"Yes, my little son; it is. I heard your sighs away off in the forest there. I know, too, why you groan like a tree cleft to the heart. I've been in the church to-day and heard how the minister has published the banns of your fair-haired sweetheart and Hans, the forest black-smith. I saw the maiden's bridal linen, too, and the gay bedstead, with its two flaming red hearts."

"Hold your tongue, woman!" growled the fisherman.

"Oho! not so hasty, my son! Choke it down.

> Slender maidens, young and sweet,
> 'Neath the moon you still may meet.

If there isn't one, there's another."

The youth covered his eyes with his hand and motioned the woman away. But the old woman did not go.

"You are my sweetheart, my own little son," she said flatteringly. "You have brought me many a supper of fish, and I have not forgotten

the otter skin you gave me for a warm hood. I
will help you, my precious lad, I will help you."

The youth suddenly jumped up. "Mother
Bridget," he said, trembling, "people say — "

"That I am a witch. No, I am not able to
anoint the tongs so that they will carry me out
at the chimney and through the air; but I know
a thing or two, my son; I know a thing or two
that few people besides myself know about, and
if you wish, I will serve you with my art."

"Can you brew a love-potion, Mother Bridget?"
asked Heini, in a whisper.

"No, but I know another little trick. And
if you do as I tell you, she will never become
his wife, for all their exchanging of rings and
getting blessed by the priest. Whenever he,
glowing with love, wishes to take his maiden to
his heart, she shall turn away from him; and
whenever she eagerly longs to twine her arms
about his neck, he shall push her away. Then
at last, if he leaves her or she grows tired of
him, she will still be yours. That I can do,
and I will teach you the spell."

"Tell me how," said Heini, in an undertone; and the old woman began to whisper in
his ear.

"Buy a steel padlock of the locksmith, and pay whatever price he asks without haggling, saying, 'In Gottes Namen.'

"Then on the day of the wedding go to the church, — pay close attention, my son, — and when the priest unites the pair at the altar, clap the lock together, saying in a low voice, 'in Teufels Namen.' Then throw the padlock into the lake, and what I have predicted will come true. Have you understood me?"

"I have understood," answered the fisherman, and a cold shiver ran down his back.

* * *

The bells were pealing from the tower, and happy people in gay holiday attire were making their way through the arched doorway of the church. The young blacksmith is to wed the beautiful Gertrude. Indeed, she is beautiful, and her yellow hair shines in the sunlight falling aslant through the window, even brighter than her bridal wreath of tinsel and glass beads. Now the choir-master takes his seat on the organ-bench; his wrinkled face beams with joy as he thinks of the wedding millet-broth, which,

according to an old custom, must be so stiff that
the spoon will stand up in it; and of the leg of
lamb, which comes after the broth. He draws
out all the stops, the mighty tones of the organ
peal through the church, and the wooden angels
over the chancel blowing trumpets puff out their
cheeks even more than usual. Then everything
is still; the minister raises his voice and ad-
dresses the couple, kneeling before the altar.
He has never before been so impressive as to-
day. The women feel after their handkerchiefs,
and here and there is heard a muffled choking
and sobbing.

Now the minister took the wedding-ring from
the plate, which stood on the altar. Then the
bride raised her eyes, but quickly dropped them
again, for she saw the fisherman Heini leaning
against a pillar. He looked deathly pale; he
held his right hand in his jacket pocket, and his
lips moved slightly. The bride no longer heard
what the minister said, neither did she hear the
congratulations of the relatives and friends who
surrounded them after the service was over.
She passed out of the church by the side of her
spouse like one who walks in a dream.

The wedding procession started toward the

bride's house, which was decorated with garlands of leaves, and on the gable stood a little
fir-tree trimmed with floating ribbons.   The
musicians took a good draught to strengthen
themselves for their approaching duties, and
soon the merry sound of violins and flutes
broke through the Sunday stillness.

In the meantime there was one who was
hastening with swift steps towards the forest.
In his heart he carried bitter pain; in his
pocket, a fastened lock.   He turned his steps
to the forest lake.   There he sat on the shore
the whole day long, holding the lock hesitatingly
in his hand.   The little gray water-wagtails
tripped along on the sand at his feet, and
looked up wonderingly at the pale youth.   The
fishes jumped up out of the water, and their
scaly coats shone like silver in the sunlight.
The blue-green dragon-flies danced over the waves
and dipped into the water.   But he paid no
attention to the little creatures.   The sun was
going down behind the ridges of the blue
mountains, the shadows were growing longer,
and still the fisherman sat brooding by the
pond.

In the distance there sounded something like

violins, and the sound came nearer and nearer.
The youth listened and gave a groan. It is
the smith leading home his bride, and the wedding guests and the musicians are escorting
them.

Heini shut his teeth together and drew out
the padlock. An owl flew past, and as he flew
his voice rang out : —

"Do it, do it, do it!" the owl seemed to say,
and the padlock made a wide arch as it fell
into the pond. Filled with terror, Heini fled
into the woods.

* * *

The magic spell which the old woman had
taught the fisherman had its effect. Instead of
the expected joy, bitter discontent entered the
home of the forest blacksmith. The newly married couple avoided each other timidly; yet if
they were separated, they were consumed with a
longing for each other: their love was blighted,
and yet their love could not die. The beautiful
Gertrude wasted away to a shadow, and the sturdy
young blacksmith, too, began to look weak and
sickly. "Somebody has bewitched them," whispered the women in the village; and many fearful
things were hinted at in the spinning-room.

The fisherman, too, seemed to be suffering from some strange malady. He wandered idly through the woods and over the fields, and avoided human beings. If the people from the village met him, they looked after him compassionately and tapped their foreheads significantly: they took the unfortunate fellow to be crazy. He was not really crazy; but bitter remorse tormented him, as he thought with a shudder of the mischief of which he had been the cause.

Finally he sought old Bridget's hut, and begged her on his knees to break the charm.

The old woman giggled. "You have a soft heart, my little son; but I will help you; I will break the charm. Procure the padlock for me. Give it a good blow with the hammer, saying, 'In Gottes Namen,' and it will break the steel padlock, and so render the charm worthless. Bring me the padlock, my treasure."

The youth struck his forehead and rushed out of the hut; and the old woman chuckled maliciously behind his back.

"Procure the padlock" kept sounding in his ears, as he again wandered restlessly through the woods; "procure the padlock." And he turned his steps towards the lake, which he had carefully avoided since he had committed that dark deed.

The evening breeze blew across the dark-green pond, and the moonlight quivered on the gently stirring waters. By the shore, on a moss-covered stone, sat the form of a woman clad in white garments. She had long, waving, yellow hair, and wore a crown of rushes and water-lilies.

"Hast thou at last come once more to my lake, thou dear child of man?" said the nixie to the fisherman; "long, long have I been waiting for thee; but I knew that thou wouldst return to me again. Come, descend to my pleasure garden, and in my arms forget those who torment thee and have taken the color out of thy rosy cheeks; forget the earth and the heavens and the sunlight." She bent towards the panting youth and twined her shining arms about his neck. "See," she continued, "I wear the pledge that thou gavest me;" and with these words she lifted the steel padlock, which hung from a coral necklace on her breast. "Thou art mine."

The fisherman seized the padlock hastily. "Give it back, give it back!" he cried; but the nixie, laughing, shook her head and wound her arms more tightly about his neck. "Come!" she whispered in his ear.

" Give me the padlock!" cried the fisherman, beseechingly; " give me the padlock, and let me go away with it for but a little while. I swear to you that I will come back to the lake this very night, and I will stay with you always. Only give me the padlock!"

The water-sprite unfastened the padlock from her necklace, saying: " Very well; I will give the pledge back to thee, but only in exchange for another. Give me one of the brown ringlets that play about thy brow."

Heini took out his knife and cut off a lock of his hair, and handed it to the water-sprite. She hid it in her dress, and gave the padlock back to the fisherman. " Forget not what thou hast promised me. I hold the curl, and hold thee by the curl. And here, take my veil. When thou returnest from thy errand, gird the veil about thy loins and step down fearlessly into the water. Down below there I will tarry for thee, my sweet beloved; down below there await thee more pleasures than there are needles in the fir forest, or drops of water in the lake. Come back quickly."

Thus spoke the water-nymph, kissed the youth on the mouth, and stepped down into the dark

water. But before she disappeared, she turned
her face once more towards her beloved, and
said warningly : " Forget not the veil, or thou
wilt be lost, and even I could not save thee
from death; forget not the veil ! "

With these words she disappeared beneath
the water; but the fisherman hurried away with
the padlock.

* * *

By the forge in the smithy sadly sat the
young blacksmith staring at the glowing coals.
The door creaked, and in walked Heini, the
fisherman. The smith greeted the belated guest
with a hostile look, and asked sharply what he
wanted.

" I have a favor to ask of you," said the
fisherman ; " let me take your heaviest hammer
for a moment."

The other looked distrustfully at his rival.
What can the crazy fellow want with a hammer? Will he try to get possession of the
woman he loves by one fell blow? But he is
enough of a man to meet an attack; so he
handed the hammer to the fisherman and seized
an iron bar to ward off the blow if it came.

The fisherman stepped up to the anvil, and

the blacksmith saw with astonishment that he laid a padlock on it.

"In Gottes Namen!" cried Heini, and lifted the hammer. It fell with a crash, and the splinters of the steel padlock flew all about the shop.

And then Heini took out of his jacket a delicate tissue and threw it on the glowing coals in the forge. A flame leaped up and in a twinkling died down again. Then he gave his hand to the blacksmith, and said in a low voice, "Farewell, and be happy!" With these words he rushed out of the door and disappeared in the darkness of the night.

The smith shook his head as he watched the crazy youth, and he stood still wrapt in thought, when two white arms were thrown about his neck, and two warm lips were lifted up to his. Laughing and weeping, his young wife clung about his neck and stammered words of love; and he lifted her with his strong arms and bore her into the house.

The red glow died away in the smithy, and a shivering man, who had been crouching breathless beneath the low window, rose and walked noiselessly away into the gloomy forest.

Good luck and happiness entered the black-smith's home, and a troop of rosy-cheeked boys and girls came to bless it.

The fisherman Heini disappeared that night, and no earthly eye ever saw him again. But the brook which flows out of the lake knows a new and dreadful tale of a dead youth, who lies at the bottom of the lake in a crystal coffin, and a beautiful water-sprite sits at his head and weeps.

THE EASTER RABBIT.

THERE was once a wealthy count who had a
beautiful wife and a little curly-haired, blue-
eyed daughter, whose name was Trudchen. Besides many other estates the count possessed an
old hunting-castle in the midst of the forest, and
the forest abounded in stags, does, and other
game.

As soon as the oak-trees began to be green, the
count came with wife and child, servant and maid,
to the forest castle and indulged in the jocund
chase till late in the autumn. Then came numerous guests from the country round, and every
day was full of gayety and pleasure.

One day there was to be a great hunt. In the
courtyard stood the saddled horses, stamping their
feet impatiently, the dogs coupled together were
tugging at the leash and could hardly be held,
and the falcons flapped their wings.

In the open doorway of the entrance-hall, which

was decorated with gigantic antlers and boars'
heads, stood Trudchen by the side of her maid,
delighting in the beautiful horses and the spotted
hounds.

Now the count with his huntsmen stepped out
into the courtyard, and Trudchen's mother followed ; she wore a long riding-dress of green velvet, and waving ostrich plumes in her hat. She
kissed Trudchen and mounted her white horse.
The count lifted up his little daughter, caressed
her, and said: '' We are going to ride in the forest, where the spotted fawns leap about, and if I
see the Easter rabbit I will give him my Trudchen's love, and tell him that next year he must
lay a nest full of bright-colored eggs for you."
And the child laughed, and kissed her father's
bearded face with her little rosy mouth. Then he
swung himself upon his raven-black horse, and the
train rode out at the castle gate. '' Frau Ursula,
take good care of the little one ! " called the count
to the maid, as he rode away, and he waved his
hand once more. Then he passed out of sight.

In the afternoon of the same day, Trudchen was
playing in the garden. Frau Ursula had twice in
succession told her the story of the ancient Easter
hare and her seven little ones, and now the good

woman was quietly sleeping on the stone bench under the linden, where the bees were humming about.

The little girl had caught a lady-bug and began to count the dots on her wings; but before she had finished, the lady-bug flew away. Trudchen ran after her until she lost sight of her. Then she saw a brown butterfly with great eyes in its wings rest-ing on a bluebell. Trudchen was just going to seize it cautiously, when all of a sudden it was gone, and on the other side of the garden wall.

Of course Trudchen could not follow him over there; but what was the gate in the wall for? The little girl stood on tip-toe and pressed down the latch, and then she was in the oak forest.

"So here is where the Easter hare dwells with her seven little ones," thought Trudchen. She hunted all about, but the little hares must live deeper in the woods. So the little girl ran on as chance led her.

She had already gone quite a little distance, and was thinking whether it would not be bet-ter to turn round, when a black and white spotted magpie flew along and stood in her way.

"Where did you get that shining chain around your neck?" said the magpie, and looked spitefully at Trudchen, with his head on one side. "Give the chain to me, or I will peck you with my bill."

The poor child was frightened, and with trembling hands she unfastened the gold chain, took it off her neck, and threw it to the magpie. He seized the ornament with his bill and flew away with it.

Now the little girl was tired of the woods. "Oh dear, my little necklace!" she sobbed; "how they will scold me at home if I go back without my chain." Trudchen turned round and ran, as she thought, back the same way that she had come; but she only got deeper into the forest.

"To-whoo! to-whoo!" sounded out of an old hollow tree; and when Trudchen looked up in affright, she saw an owl glaring at her with great, fiery eyes, and cracking his crooked bill. "To-whoo!" said the owl, "where did you get that beautiful veil on your head? Give the veil to me, or I will scratch you with my claws."

Trudchen trembled like an aspen leaf. She threw down the veil and ran as fast as she could. But the owl took the veil and put it over his face.

Again the child wandered aimlessly about the

forest. Twisted roots like brown snakes crossed her path, and the briers tore Trudchen's dress with their thorny claws. There was a rustling in the top of a tree, and a red squirrel skipped down on the trunk.

"That will do me no harm," thought the little one; but there she was mistaken; the squirrel was not one whit better than the magpie or the owl.

"Ah! what a beautiful little hood you have," it said; "it would make a soft, warm nest for my young ones. Give the hood to me, or I will bite you with my sharp teeth."

Then the little girl gave away her hood, and continued her wandering, weeping bitterly. Her feet could hardly carry her another step, but her distress impelled her on.

Now the woods grew light, and Trudchen came to a sunny meadow. Bluebells and red pinks grew in the grass, and gay butterflies danced in the air. But Trudchen never thought of catching the butterflies, or gathering the flowers. She sat down on the grass, and wept and sobbed enough to melt the heart of a stone.

Then there came out of the woods an old man with a long gray beard. He wore on his head a broad-brimmed hat with a wide band, and he carried a white staff in his hand. Behind him flew two ravens.

There was a rushing sound in the tops of the oaks, and trees, bushes, and flowers all bowed down.

The man came straight to Trudchen, stood still in front of her, and asked in a gentle voice, "Why are you weeping, my child?"

Trudchen felt confidence in the old man, and told him who she was, and what the wicked creatures had done to her.

"Never mind, Trudchen," said the old man, kindly. "I will send you home." He beckoned to the ravens. They flew on his shoulder, and listened attentively to the words which the old man spoke to them. Then they spread their wings and flew away as swift as arrows.

It was not long before they came back again; but they brought something with them. It was a stork.

When the stork saw the old man with the broad hat, he bowed so low that the end of his red bill touched the ground, and then he stood meekly like a slave, awaiting his master's command.

And the old man said: "Beloved and trusted Master Adebar, you see here a lost child. Do you know where her home is?"

The stork looked closely at the child, then he clapped his bill together with joy, and said: "Yes, to be sure, Herr Wode, I know the child, for I brought her myself to the count's castle four years ago."

"Very well," said the man; "then carry her there once more."

The stork moved his neck thoughtfully to and fro. "That would be a hard piece of work," he replied.

"It must be," said the old man. "Have you not often carried twins and even triplets in your bill? Quickly to work, or we are friends no more."

"Certainly; if it is your command, I must obey," replied the stork, submissively, and seized the child around the waist with his bill.

"But my little chain, my veil, and my hood," bewailed Trudchen.

"My ravens shall take them away from the wicked creatures and bring them back to you," said the old man, comfortingly. "Master Stork, fulfil your task faithfully."

The man nodded kindly to Trudchen, and in a moment she felt herself lifted up, and the stork bore her through the air.

Oh, they went like the wind! Trudchen looked down and saw the forest far below her like a bed of curly parsley. Then sight and hearing left her.

When Trudchen came back to consciousness, and opened her eyes, she was lying in the grass in the castle garden, and Frau Ursula was standing before her, chiding her: —

"Child, child, lying here asleep in the damp grass! If you catch cold, it will be again, 'Old Ursula doesn't take any care at all of the child'—and I haven't taken my eyes off from you. And there is your beautiful gold necklace lying in the middle of the path, and there lies your hood, and your veil is hanging by a thorn on the rose-bush. Get up and come into the house with me; it is growing cold in the garden. Oh, dear Heaven, what anxiety you put upon me!"

And Trudchen got up and let her scold on, without opening her mouth.

How fortunate that Frau Ursula did not know all that had taken place! That would have made a fine commotion.

THE GOLDEN TREE.

THE room in which our story begins was
very plain and bare. Against the white-
washed walls, whose only adornment was a pair
of landscapes yellow with age, stood two small
beds, a bookcase, and a clothes-press, on the top
of which rested a terrestrial globe. A long
table, covered with ink-stains, occupied the middle of the room, and two boys about twelve
years of age were sitting by it on hard wooden
stools.

The light-haired boy was puzzling over a
difficult passage in Cornelius Nepos, and he
sighed as he turned the leaves of the heavy
lexicon; the boy with brown hair was trying
to extract the cubic root of a number with
nine figures. The Latin student was named
Hans, the mathematician Heinz.

From time to time the boys raised their
heads and looked longingly towards the open

window, where the flies buzzed in and out. In
the garden, the golden sunshine lay on the
trees and bushes, and the branch of a blossoming elder-bush looked scornfully into the two
young fellows' study. The poor youths had still
an hour to sit and bear the heat before they
could go out-doors, and the minutes crept along
like the snails on the gooseberry-bushes in the
garden. Any escape from work before the time
was not to be thought of, for in the next room,
at his desk, sat Dr. Schlagen, who had charge
of the boys' education and morals, and the door
stood open, so that the Doctor could at any time
assure himself of the presence of his charges,
and overlook whatever they were doing.

" Hannibal could not have done anything more
prudent than to cross the Alps," snarled Hans;
and " nine times eighty-one are seven hundred and
twenty-nine," muttered Heinz, in a dull voice.
Then both looked up from their work, looked at
one another and yawned.

Suddenly they heard a loud buzzing. A rose-
bug which must have alighted on the elderberry-
bush, had strayed into the room. Three times it
flew around the boys' heads, in a circle, and then it
fell plump into the inkstand.

" It really served him right," said Heinz; " why didn't he stay where he was well off ? But to be drowned in ink — that is too wretched a death ! Wait a minute, my friend, I will save you."

He was going to help the struggling bug with his penholder, but Hans accomplished the rescue more quickly with his finger. And then the boys dried the poor little rascal gently with the blotting-paper, and watched him make his toilet with his forelegs.

" He has a red spot on his breast, and black horns," said Hans, as he wiped his ink-stained fingers on his hair. " It is the king of the rose-bugs. He dwells in a castle built of jasmine flowers and shingled with rose-leaves. Crickets and locusts are his musicians, and the glowworms are his torch-bearers."

" Oh, nonsense ! " said Heinz.

" And whoever meets the king of the rose-bugs," continued Hans, " is a lucky fellow. Take heed, Heinz, something is going to happen — an adventure or something extraordinary, and besides, to-day is May-day, so there is a special reason for expecting wonders. See how he beckons to us with his feelers, and lifts his wings. Now he is going to be changed before us into an elf wearing a king's mantle and a golden helmet on his head."

"He is going to fly away," said Heinz, laughing. "Buzz — there he goes."

The boys went to the window and looked after the bug. The bright little jewel made a wide circle as he flew through the air and disappeared the other side of the garden wall. Just at this moment a hemming was heard in the next room, and the two scholars hurried back to their books.

"There is our wonder," whispered Hans to his companion, and pointed to the inkstand.

Out of the inkstand rose a green shoot that grew while they were looking at it, and mounted to the ceiling.

"We are dreaming," said Heinz, rubbing his eyes.

"No; it is a fairy tale," said Hans, exultingly; "a living fairy tale, and we are in it."

And the shoot grew larger and put forth branches and twigs with leaves and blossoms. The top of the room disappeared, the walls vanished, and the astonished boys found themselves in the midst of a dim wood.

"Come along!" cried Hans, pulling the reluctant Heinz away with him. "Now comes the adventure."

The blossoming shrubs separated of themselves
and made a path for the boys. The broken sunlight looked through the latticed roof of the trees
and painted a thousand golden spots on the moss,
and out of the moss grew star-flowers of glowing
colors, and green curling tendrils twined about
their mossy stems. Above in the branches fluttered singing birds with bright feathers, and stags,
roebucks, and other game leaped gayly about
among the bushes.

Now the woods grew light, and something like
firelight shone between the trunks of the trees, and
Hans whispered to his companion, "Now it is
coming!"

They came to a meadow in the wood, in the
midst of which stood a single tree. But it was no
ordinary tree; it was the magic tree of which
Hans had so often heard, — the tree with golden
leaves. The boys stood still in amazement.

Out from behind the trunk stepped a dwarf no
larger than a child of three years, but not with the
large head and flat feet that dwarfs usually have,
but slender and graceful. He wore a green cloak
and a golden helmet, and the two boys knew who
he was.

The dwarf advanced two steps and made a low

bow. "The enchanted princess is waiting for her deliverer," he said; "which of you will undertake the hazardous task?"

"I," said Hans, in a joyful voice. And the dwarf immediately led out a little milk-white steed, champing a golden bit.

"Don't do it, Hans!" said Heinz, in distress; but Hans was already seated in the saddle. The magic horse rose, neighing, into the air, then he threw back his head and ran with flying mane into the woods. A bright rose-bug flew along ahead as guide. Once only Hans turned his head and looked at his comrade standing beneath the golden tree; then both tree and friend were lost from sight.

That was a merry ride. Hans sat as safe and sure in the saddle as though he had been on his accustomed wooden stool instead of the horse's back. When he thought how only an hour ago he had been groaning over Cornelius Nepos and trembling before Doctor Schlagen, he had to laugh. The little schoolboy in a short jacket had become a stately huntsman with waistcoat and mantle, sword and golden spear. So away he flew through the magic forest.

Now his little steed neighed gladly. The woods

grew light. A leap or two more, and horse and
rider stopped before a shining castle. Gay banners waved from the towers, horns and trumpets
were sounding, and on the balcony stood the princess waving a white handkerchief. She looked
exactly like the neighbor's little Helen, with whom
Hans the Knight used to play when he was a little
boy, and still at school, only she was larger and a
thousand times more beautiful.

Hans sprang from the saddle, and with clink-
ing spurs hastened up the marble steps. In the
open doorway stood a man, probably the mar-
shal of the princess' household, who had a very
familiar look to our Hans.

And the house-marshal reached out his hand,
seized Hans the Knight by the ear, and cried: —

"The scoundrel has gone to sleep. Just wait
till I —" That broke the spell. Hans was sitting once more by the ink-stained table; before
him lay Cornelius Nepos and the Latin lexicon;
opposite him sat Heinz, writing with a squeak-
ing pen; and near him stood Doctor Schlagen,
looking sternly through his spectacles at the
dreamer.

When the hour at last struck for their release,
and the two boys were eating their evening meal

out in the garden under the elder-tree, Hans told his friend what he had dreamed.

"That is strange," said Heinz, when Hans had finished; "very strange. For I had the same dream myself, only the ending was different; no magic castle came into my dream—"

"Tell me about it!" urged Hans.

"As far as the golden tree, my dream was exactly like yours. You mounted the white horse and rode away to release the princess. But I—"

"Well?" said Hans, impatiently.

"I remained behind, shook the tree, and filled all my pockets with the golden leaves. Then the stupid old doctor woke me up, and then the splendid dream was over."

"Heinz," said Hans, solemnly, seizing his friend by the hand, "if two people have the very same dream, then it will surely come true. The dream was a prophecy. Remember what I say."

Then the boys ate the rest of their supper and went to play ball.

Was the dream of the boys ever fulfilled? Yes. Hans became a poet, and drove his steed through the green forest of fairyland. But Heinz, who shook the golden tree in the dream, became his publisher.

THE MAGIC BOW.

ONCE there was a little boy whose name was
Frieder, and who had neither father nor
mother. He was as handsome as a picture, and
when he was playing in front of the house in
the street, people would stop and ask, "Whose
little one is that?" Then the surly old woman
who brought him up on thin broth and plentiful
scoldings would answer, "He is nobody's child;
and it would be the best thing for him if the
dear Lord would take him to himself in his heavenly kingdom." But Frieder had no longing
for the heavenly kingdom; it pleased him very
well down below here, and he grew up like the
red-headed thistles behind his foster-mother's
house. Playfellows he had none. When the
other boys in the village built mills and sailed
their little canoes in the brook, or romped in the
hay, Frieder would sit on the hillside and whistle
the songs of the birds.

He was busying himself in this way one day, when old Klaus, who was a bird-catcher by profession, met him. He took a fancy to the pretty lad, and struck a friendship with him. From that time the two were often seen sitting sociably together in front of the bird-catcher's cottage like two old soldiers. Klaus not only could tell strange stories of the forest, but he knew how to play the fiddle, and instructed Frieder in the art, after giving him an old patched-up violin as a birthday present. The pupil did his teacher credit, for before the end of the month he could play several famous old melodies. The old bird-catcher was deeply impressed by this, and said prophetically, " Frieder, believe me ; if God spares my life, I shall sometime see you the first violinist in the church."

When Frieder was fifteen years old, the neighbors came together and took counsel about him. It was time, they said, that he should learn something practical to help him through the world; and when they asked him what he would like to become, he answered, " A musician." Then the people threw up their hands in holy horror. But a stout man stepped out of the crowd, grasped the lad's hand, and said in a dignified manner,

"I will see if I can make something practical out of him." And all those who stood about in the circle thought Frieder very fortunate to have found such a master.

He was a person of no little consequence. He cut the peasants' hair and beards, cupped them, and pulled out their poor teeth, and often their sound ones too. He was the barber of the place, and the people called him nothing less than "Herr Doktor."

On the same day Frieder went to the house of him who was now his employer, and in the evening began to make himself useful by bringing his master's beer from the ale-house. By degrees he learned to make the lather, to hone the razors, and to do everything else belonging to the art. His master was pleased with him; but the violin-playing in which Frieder had indulged so eagerly when he had nothing else to do, was objectionable to him, for, in the barber's opinion, it belonged to the unprofitable arts.

Two long years passed by. Then came the day when Frieder was to put his skill to the test. If he succeeded in satisfying his master, then he could go out into the world as a travelling journeyman and seek his fortune. He was to prove his skill by shaving his master's beard, and that was no joke.

The important day had come.   The barber seated himself in his chair, with the white towel around his neck, and leaned his head back. Frieder soaped his double chin, stropped the razor, and fell to work.

Suddenly the sounds of violins and flutes were heard in front of the house: a bear-leader had come along.   As soon as the young barber heard the music his hand slipped, and on the master's cheek appeared a bloody cut, reaching from his ear to his nose.

Alas for poor Frieder!   The chair in which the barber was sitting fell backwards on the floor.   The bleeding man jumped up in a rage and gave his apprentice a rousing box on the ear.   Then he tore open the door, pointed into the blue air, and screamed, "Go to the cuckoo!"

Then Frieder packed up his things, took his violin under his arm, and went to the cuckoo. The cuckoo dwelt in the woods, in an oak-tree, and happened to be at home when Frieder called on him.   He heard the fellow's account patiently to the end, but then he flapped his wings, and said : —

"Young friend, if I should help all who are sent to me, I should have a great deal to do. The times are hard, and I must be glad that I have provided for my own children tolerably well. The oldest I have boarded out in a water-wagtail's family; the second one, neighbor red-tail has taken into his house; the third child, a little maid, is nursed by an old beam-bird; and the two smallest ones are taken care of by a wren. I have to bestir myself from morning till night in order to get enough to live on decently. For fourteen days I have lived on hairy caterpillars, and such food would not suit your digestion. No; I cannot help you, however sorry I may be for you."

Then Frieder hung his head sorrowfully, said farewell to the cuckoo, and went away. But he had not gone far when the cuckoo called after him: "Wait, Frieder! I have a good idea. Perhaps I can help you after all. Come with me." He spoke these words, stretched his wings, and flew along in front of Frieder to show him the way.

Frieder had difficulty in following his guide, for the underbrush was thick in the woods, and the briers were very abundant. At last it grew

light between the trees, and there was a glimpse
of water.

"This is the place," said the cuckoo, as he
lighted on an alder. Before the youth lay a
dark-green pond, fed by a foaming waterfall.
Reeds and iris grew on the shore, and white
water-lilies with broad leaves floated on the surface.

"Now pay attention," said the wise bird.
"When the sun goes down and makes the spray
of the waterfall gleam in seven colors, then
Neck comes up from the bottom of the pond
where he has a crystal castle, and sits down
on the shore. Then have no fear, but speak
to him. You will find out the rest."

Then Frieder thanked the cuckoo, who flew
away swiftly into the woods.

When the seven colors of the rainbow appeared in the waterfall, sure enough Neck came
up out of the water. He had on a little red
coat and a white collar. His hair was green,
and hung down like a tangled mane over his
shoulders. He sat down on a stone, which rose
above the mirror-like pond, let his feet hang in
the water, and began to comb his hair with his
ten fingers. This was a difficult task, for the

snarls were full of eel-grass, duckweed, and little snail-shells, and as Neck tried to smooth out his hair he made up painful faces.

"This is the right time to speak to the water-sprite," thought Frieder. He took courage, stepped out from the alder-bushes, which had kept him from sight, took off his hat, and said, "Good evening, Herr Neck!"

At the sound of his voice, Neck plumped into the water like a startled frog, and disappeared. But before long he thrust his head out again, and said in an unfriendly voice, "What do you want?"

"With your permission, Herr Neck," began Frieder, "I am an experienced barber, and you would confer a great honor upon me if you would allow me to comb your hair."

"Indeed!" said Neck, delighted, and he rose out of the water. "You have come at just the right time. What a trouble and torment my hair has been to me since the Loreley, my cousin, was mean enough to leave me! What have I not done for that thankless creature! And one morning she went away, and my golden comb is gone, too, and now she sits, as I hear, on a rock in the Rhine, and is having some trouble with a skipper in a little skiff. The golden comb will soon be sung away."

With these words, Neck sat down on a stone. Frieder took out his shaving-case, tied a white apron around the water-sprite's neck, and combed and oiled his hair, till it was as smooth as silk; then he parted his hair evenly from his brow to the nape of his neck, took off the apron, and made a bow, as his master had taught him. Neck stood up and looked at himself with satisfaction in the mirror of the pond. "What do I owe you?" he asked.

Frieder had the customary answer, "Whatever you please," on his lips, but it occurred to him just in time that he must seize the opportunity and strike while the iron was hot. So he cleared his throat and told Neck his history.

"So you would like to be a musician?" asked Neck, when Frieder had finished speaking. "Just take your fiddle in your hand and let me hear something of your skill."

Then the youth took his violin, tuned the strings, and played his best piece, "When the Grandfather married the Grandmother," and when he had ended with a graceful flourish, he looked expectantly at Neck.

Neck grinned, and said, "Now hear me." Then he put his hand down into the reeds and brought out a violin and bow, straightened himself up, and began to play.

Poor Frieder had never heard anything like it before. At first it sounded like the evening breeze playing among the rushes, then it sounded like the roar of a waterfall, and at last, like gently flowing water. The birds in the trees were silent, the bees stopped humming, and the fishes raised their heads out of the pond to listen to the sweet sounds. But great tears shone in the young fellow's eyes.

"Herr Neck," he said, stretching out his hands, as the water-sprite laid down his bow, "Herr Neck, teach me how to play!"

"That would not do," answered Neck. "It would not do on account of my growing daughters, the nixies. Besides, it isn't necessary. If you will give me your comb, you shall have a violin that hasn't its equal."

"I will give you my whole shaving-case, if you want it," cried Frieder, and handed it to the water-sprite.

Neck snatched the proffered case quickly, and disappeared beneath the water.

"Hold on, hold on!" the youth called after him, but his call was in vain. He waited an hour; he waited two; but nothing more was heard of Neck.

Poor Frieder sighed deeply, for it was plain to him that the false water-sprite had deceived him, and with a heavy heart he turned to go he knew not where. Then he saw lying at his feet, on the edge of the pond, Neck's fiddlestick. He bent down, and as he took it in his hand, he felt a twitching from the tips of his fingers to his shoulder-blade, and it urged him to try the bow.

He was going to play "What shall I, poor fellow, do?" but it seemed as if an unseen power guided his hand; sweet, silvery tones burst from his violin, such as Frieder had never heard in his life but once, and that was just before, when Neck was playing to him. The birds came flying along and sat listening in the bushes, the fishes leaped up out of the water, and stags and roebucks came out of the forest, and looked with wise eyes at the player. Frieder could not tell how it happened. Whatever passed through his soul and whatever he felt in his heart, found its way to his hand, and through his hand to his playing, and was expressed in sweet tones.

But Neck came up out of the pond and nodded approvingly. Then he disappeared and was never seen again.

Frieder went out of the forest playing, and he visited all the kingdoms of the earth and played before kings and emperors. Yellow gold rained into his hat, and he would have become exceeding rich, if he had not been a true musician. But true musicians never become rich.

He left his shaving-case behind him. Therefore, he let his hair grow like strong Samson of old. Other musicians have followed his example, and from that time to the present day have worn long, disorderly hair.

THE BEECH-TREE.

———◦◇◦———

THERE stood in the forest an ancient beech-
tree. The top of the tree had been shattered by the lightning, her side was hollow, and
great mushrooms grew out of the bark. She
was the oldest of all beeches, and the mother of
a numerous family; but she had seen all her
children, as soon as they had grown strong, fall
beneath the stroke of the axe, and she had only
one daughter left. She was a young beech, with
smooth bark and a heaven-aspiring crown, and
she was just eighty years old. This is considered the prime of life among the forest trees.

Every spring the old beech still put forth
leaves and green shoots, but she felt that life
was on the decline with her, for it was only
with difficulty that she held herself upright.
And because she felt that she must die, her love
for her beautiful giant daughter was redoubled.

Spring was drawing near. The glistening

white snow still lay on the branches of the trees, but the warm sap began to spring up from the roots, and the soft air blew and helped to melt the snow. The crackling ice-cakes floated down the rivers and brooks, the willows pushed their silver catkins out of their cases, and the white bell-flowers broke through the vanishing carpet of snow that covered the forest floor.

Then the old beech said to her child: "To-night the warm south wind will come with a rush. It will lay me on the bed of leaves that I have been hoarding up all these years, and I shall return to the mother earth, from whose bosom I came forth. But before I go home, I will bequeath you a legacy that the gentle lord of the forest bestowed upon me one day a long time ago, when he was resting from his blessed labors in my shadow. You will be able to understand the words and deeds of men and to sympathize in their joys and sorrows. This is the highest good that can fall to our lot. But be prepared to see more of pain than happiness."

Thus spoke the old beech-tree, and gave her daughter her blessing.

In the night the south wind came rushing
from the desert. It buried the ships in the bil-
lows of the sea, rolled gigantic snowballs down
from the mountains, and destroyed men's cot-
tages as it passed by. It went roaring through
the forest and broke down everything that was
old and decayed, or whatever dared to resist its
power. It stretched the old beech on the
ground, and shook her sturdy daughter, but she
wisely bent and bowed her head, and the mighty
wind passed over. For three days the daughter
wept tears of sparkling dew over her mother.
Then the sun came and dried her tears.

And now on every side began such a budding
and sprouting that the beech had no time to
mourn. Her buds swelled and burst, and one
morning a hundred thousand little tender green
leaves trembled in the warm sunshine. What a
delight it was!

Golden yellow primroses came up out of the
ground. They did not even take time to push
aside the dry leaves, but pierced right through
them and lifted themselves up once more into
the sunlight. Purple peas joined the primroses,
and the fragrant woodroof unrolled its tender
querl of leaves. What exuberance of life!

And in the midst of all this blooming life stood the young beech like a queen. A finch had built his nest in her crest and the woodpecker with his red cap came to visit her. Once the cuckoo came too, and even the distinguished squirrel, with his bushy tail over his head, found his way there now and then, although the beech with her bright spring foliage could not serve him with acorns. But she had not yet seen a human being this spring, and they were the guests she most wished to see, because she possessed the gift of understanding their sayings and doings.

Human beings were soon to come. One morning a slender young maiden, with long brown braids of hair, came tripping along through the forest and went straight up to the beech-tree. But there was not the least probability that she had come on account of the beech. She looked at the tree that lay mouldering on the ground, and said, " This is the place." Then she put down her basket, which was filled with lilies-of-the-valley, and leaned against the beech, without even glancing at the green splendor above. The tree held her breath to listen to what the maiden might say, but the beautiful girl kept an obstinate silence.

Then from the opposite direction came a

stately youth. He wore a little round hat with a
curling feather, like a huntsman's. Cautiously he
crept along, so cautiously that the dry leaves never
once rustled beneath his footsteps. But although
he stepped so gently, the maiden's sharp ears per-
ceived his coming. She turned her head toward
him, and the beech-tree thought to herself, "Now
she will run away." But the maiden did not run
away; she rather sprang toward the youth and
threw her arms around his brown neck.

"My Hans!"—"My Eva!" they cried at the
same time. Then they kissed each other to their
hearts' content, called each other again by name,
and embraced each other anew, and the beech-tree
found it very tiresome. Afterwards they sat down
under the tree and talked of their love. It was
the old, old story, but it was new to the beech, and
she listened as a child listens to a fairy tale. But
something still more strange happened to surprise her.

The youth rose from the ground, took out his
knife, and began to cut into the bark on the trunk.
Indeed it caused her some pain, but the tree held
as still as a wall.

"What is it going to be?" asked the maiden.

"A heart, with your name and mine," replied
Hans, and went on cutting.

When the work was done, they both looked at it with satisfaction, and the beech was as pleased as one whom the king has honored with a golden chain. "Human beings are capital people!" she thought.

Then the youth began to sing. The beech had long known the songs of the finches and black-birds by heart; now she was going to hear something quite different from the songs of the birds. The song ran thus: —

Behind the forest cover
I strode the wild path over, —
The air was cool and clear.
I left the young fawn browsing,
Nor stags nor red roes rousing,
I sought a different kind of deer.

My search was soon rewarded;
I' the shade a beech accorded
I found my love alone.
She threw her arms around me
And with caresses crowned me —
My rival's heart was turned to stone.

Upon the beech-tree hoary,
A symbol of our story,
A single heart I grave.
And there our hearts united
Shall tell of true love plighted
As long as forest trees shall wave.

"Listen, Hans!" said the maiden, when the youth had ended. "Your song reminds me of something. I know — the people say that in the autumn you go secretly after game in the forest. Let hunting alone! The forester has a grudge against you anyway—you know why. And if he should meet you as a poacher in the forest, then — oh, my Hans, if they should bring you home shot through the heart—"

The young fellow bent down over the maiden, who leaned caressingly against his shoulder, and kissed her mouth. "The people tell many things. Don't believe all that people say, my dear heart's love!" Then he threw his arm around her waist, and went away singing with her into the woods.

When the pair had disappeared behind the trees, a man in hunting-dress, with a rifle on his back and a huntsman's knife at his side, leaped out of the bushes. His face was pale and distorted. He walked up to the beech and looked at the heart which Hans had cut in the bark. He laughed wildly, and took out his knife to erase the names; but he changed his mind, and thrust the blade back into its sheath. He shook his fist threateningly in the direction which the lovers had taken, and grinding his teeth, said: "If I meet you once more poaching in the forest, then you will have heard the cuckoo's call for the last time."

With these words he went into the woods, and the tree shook her head with displeasure.

* * *

In the course of the summer the beech saw many human beings, — poor women, who gathered leaves or dry branches; children, picking berries; forest-folk, and travellers. But the most welcome guests to her shady roof were the youth and the maiden with the brown braids. They came once a week, spoke of their love, and embraced each other; and the beech grew more and more fond of them every day.

One morning before sunrise, when the forest mountain still had on its gray hood of mist, Hans came alone. He carried a rifle by a leather strap, and walked carefully through the underbrush — as carefully as though he wished to surprise his sweetheart. But this time his coming was not to meet the beautiful Eva, but the stag, which had his haunt here. At the foot of the beech-tree the youth stopped and stood as motionless as though he were a tree himself. The cool

morning breeze came and blew the mist down
in streaks. The birds awoke and flew away
after water. There was a stirring in the underbrush of the forest, and Hans lifted his gun.

There came a shot out of the thicket. Hans
dropped his rifle, leaped up, and then fell on the
ground.

Out of the forest, with hasty bounds, came a
man, carrying a smoking gun in his left hand.
The beech knew him well.

The forester bent over the fallen man. "It
is all over with him," he said. Then he loaded
his rifle and disappeared in the thicket.

The sun rose and shone on the pale face of
a dead man. The tree bent down her branches
mournfully, and wept shining tears. The robin-
redbreast flew along and put flowers on the
dead youth's face, till his glassy eyes were entirely covered over.

In the afternoon the wood-cutters came along
the path and found the corpse.

"He was shot while poaching," they said.
Then they lifted him up and carried him down
into the valley.

An old man lingered by the tree. He took
his knife and cut a cross in the bark. He put

it directly over the heart. Then he took off his hat and said a prayer.

There was a rustling in the top of the beech; the tree also was praying after her fashion.

For many summers in succession the murdered youth's sweetheart came on the day of his death to the beech-tree, knelt down, and wept and prayed; and every time she looked paler and more languid. Finally she came no more.

"She must be dead," said the beech; and so she was.

* * *

Years had passed, and the beech had grown to a mighty tree. Her bark was covered with brownish moss; vines of woodbine climbed up the trunk, and both heart and cross were covered over with green.

One day there came a man, who added a third mark to the other two; and the beech knew what it signified. The tree was marked to be cut down.

Farewell, thou verdant, delectable forest!

It was not long before the wood-cutters came, and their axes cut the beech-tree to the heart. A sullen-looking man in hunting-dress, with gray beard and hair, directed the wood-cutters.

The beech knew the man right well, and the man seemed to recognize the tree. He went up to her and tore the moss and ivy-tresses away from her trunk, so that the cross and heart became visible.

"Here it was," he said in an undertone; and his limbs shook with horror.

"Back, forester, back!" screamed the woodcutters. "The tree will fall."

The forester staggered back, but it was too late. The beech fell with a crash to the ground, and buried him under her boughs.

When they took him out, he was dead. The beech had shattered his head.

And the men stood around in a circle and prayed.

THE WATER OF FORGETFULNESS.

IN the round tower-room adorned with hunting
equipments, antlers, and stuffed wild birds, sat
a youth on a wooden stool, twisting a bow-string
out of marten-sinews and singing a gay hunting
song. His dress indicated that he was a huntsman; his short hair that he was a servant in the
castle. His name was Heinz.

From the ceiling above the young fellow's head
hung a swinging hoop, and in the hoop sat a gray
falcon, with his wings tied and the hood over his
eyes. From time to time the huntsman would
stop his work and set the hoop which was gradually coming to a halt in quick motion again.
This was to prevent the falcon from going to
sleep, for it was a young bird and was to be
trained for hunting: the breaking-in of a properly
trained falcon begins with making him submissive
through hunger and sleeplessness.

Heinz had been the count's falconer, and the

old master had kept the youth busy all the time.
But now better days had come to him. The count
hunted no longer, for he had been lying silent and
still, a whole year, in a stone coffin decorated with
coats-of-arms; and his widow, Frau Adelheid, sat
the whole day long with the chaplain and gave no
thought to hunting affairs.

To-day the mistress of the castle must have
been tired of praying, for she came out of her
apartments and wandered through the rooms of
the fortress. The young fellow's song made a
pleasing contrast to the monotonous, nasal chant-
ing of the chaplain; she followed the voice, and
entered the falconer's room in the tower.

Heinz looked amazed when he saw the proud
lady in her mourning veil and gray dress coming
in. He rose and made a low, respectful bow.
Frau Adelheid's brilliant eyes scanned the falconer's slender form, and she smiled graciously,
and her smile seemed to the youth like May sunshine. The lady asked many questions about
falconry and the chase; and when she took her
departure, she gave the huntsman such a strange
look that the bold lad turned his head on one
side like a little fourteen-year-old girl.

A few days afterwards it chanced that Frau

Adelheid rode into the green forest on a milk-
white palfrey. She wore no gray clothes, however,
but a dress of green velvet, and instead of the
widow's veil, a sable-skin hat with curling feathers.
Behind her rode Heinz, the young falconer, with
the falcon on his wrist; and his blue eyes shone
with delight.

They had already ridden some distance, and
the castle-tower had long before disappeared behind the widespreading branches of the beeches.
Then Frau Adelheid turned her head and said,
"Ride by my side, Heinz." And Heinz did as
the lady commanded him. The path was narrow,
and the countess' riding-dress brushed against the
falconer's knee. Thus they rode along. The trees
rustled softly, the chaffinches sang, and occasionally
little forest creatures scampered across the path.
Now and then there was a crackling of breaking
branches, as some deer hastened into the woods,
or a startled bird flew up with fluttering wings,
and then deep silence lay over the forest again.
And the lady of the castle turned her head a
second time to the huntsman, and said, with a
smile on her lips : —

"Now let me see, Heinz, whether you are a
well-trained huntsman.

" 'Dear huntsman, tell me aright
What mounts higher than falcon and kite ? ' "

Without stopping to think, Heinz replied : —

" High mounts the hawk, and high mounts the kite,
But the eagle takes a loftier flight."

And Frau Adelheid asked again : —

" Dear huntsman, tell me true,
What mounts higher than the eagle too? "

The falconer thought a moment or two, then
he answered : —

" Still higher than all the birds that fly
Mounts the bright sun-ball in the sky."

The countess nodded with satisfaction, and
asked for the third time : —

" Declare it to me, beloved one,
What mounts still higher than the light of the sun ? "

Now the falconer's skill was at an end. He
looked up to the tops of the trees, as if help might
come to him from there, and then he looked down
at the pommel of his saddle ; but he had nothing
to say.

Then Frau Adelheid reined in her palfrey, bent
towards the huntsman, and said in a low voice : —

"The sun mounts high in the heavens above;
But higher still mounts secret love."

She spoke these words, and threw her white
arms about the lad's neck, and kissed his dark
cheeks.

Two nutcrackers, with blue wings, fluttered
out of the hazel bushes and flew screaming into
the woods to tell what they had seen; and the
next morning the sparrows, which had their nests
under the castle roof, twittered one to another: —

"Tweet, tweet,
The lady's love for the hunter 's sweet."

Indeed, it was a fine time for falconer Heinz.
He let his hair grow till it hung in yellow ringlets down over his shoulders, and he wore silver
spurs and a heron's feather in his hat, and he
built castles in the air, each one more glowing
than the last.

To be sure he owned no castles, but he was
invested with a splendid forest lodge with antlers
on the gable, and field and meadow land, and
there he lived now as forester, and when his
gracious lady came riding out to him, he would
stand in the doorway and wave his hat to greet
her, then lift Frau Adelheid down from the

saddle, and entertain her with bread, milk, and honey.

Thus the summer passed away, and the autumn, and half the winter, and it came to be Shrovetide. Then there was a great deal of visiting in the neighborhood, and the count's castle looked like an inn. But forester Heinz sat lonely in the huntsman's house, and only occasionally did the report of the merry doings at the castle come to his ears. Finally came news that was not altogether pleasing to poor Heinz. Frau Adelheid was to be married again, so the story went; and it fell on the young fellow's ear like a funeral bell.

Then Heinz closed the door of his house and went on the way to the castle, muttering between his teeth all sorts of things that sounded not like prayers.

When he came to the foot of the mountain, where the winding road leads up to the castle, he heard the sound of hoofs, and a laugh as clear as silver, that cut his heart like a two-edged knife; and down the path came the lady of the castle on her white palfrey, and near her a handsome gentleman, richly dressed, bestrode a sleek black horse, and gazed with sparkling eyes at the beautiful woman by his side.

Then it seemed to the young forester as though his heart would burst; but he controlled himself. He sat down on a stone, like a beggar, and as the pair drew near to him, he sang : —

"The sun mounts high in the heavens above;
  But higher still mounts secret love."

The haughty knight reined in his steed, pointed with his whip at the huntsman, and asked his companion, "What does that mean? Who is the man?"

The color left the countess' cheeks, but she quickly recovered herself, and said : —

"A crazy huntsman. Come, let us hurry past him. It frightens me to be near him."

But the knight had opened his purse, and he threw a gold piece to the man by the wayside. Then Heinz cried aloud, and threw himself face downwards on the ground. But the riders spurred on their horses and rode hastily away.

The sound of the hoofs had long died away before the unfortunate youth rose from the ground. He wiped the dust and dirt from his face, pulled his hat down over his eyes, and strode away into the forest. He hurried on aimlessly till night-fall. Then he threw himself down under a tree,

wrapped his cloak about him, and sleep came
over the exhausted man.

Poor Heinz slept all night long without a
dream, till the chill of dawn awoke him. But
immediately his whole sorrow stood again before
him and grinned at him like an evil spirit.

"Oh, if I could forget," he cried; "if I could
only forget! There is a fountain, and if one
drinks of its waters all the past vanishes from
his memory. Who will show me the way to
that spring?"

"Here!" called a voice near at hand. "The
water that causes forgetfulness I am very familiar
with, and I will gladly tell you all that I know
about it."

Heinz looked up and saw before him a youth
in dark, tattered garments; his toes peeped in-
quisitively out of his shoes. He represented himself to be a travelling scholar, and went on to
say : —

"The water which makes one forget is called
Lethe, and has its source in Greece. You will
have to take a journey there and inquire the
particulars on the spot. But if you wish to have
it more conveniently, come with me to the tavern
of the Purple Grape. It is not far from here.

There the hostess will give you a taste of the
water of forgetfulness, provided that your purse
is longer than mine."

These were the scholar's words. Heinz arose
and followed him to the forest inn. There they
drank together all one day and half the night; and
when, towards midnight, they lay peaceably on
the bench, Heinz had forgotten everything that
troubled and oppressed him. But with the morning light the tormenting recollection returned, and
he had a headache besides. Then he paid his own
bill and his companion's, took a hasty farewell of
the travelling scholar, and went on further.

"Oh, who could forget!" he said as he went
along, and beat his forehead with his fist. "I
must find the fountain, or I shall be really insane."

By the wayside stood an old half-dead willow,
and in the willow sat a raven, who turned his head
toward the lonely wanderer and looked at him
with curiosity.

"Thou wise bird," said the forester to the
raven, "thou knowest everything that happens
on the earth; tell me, where does the water of
forgetfulness flow?"

"I, too, should like to know that," said the
raven, "in order to drink of it myself. I knew a

nest with seven fat, nut-fed dormice, and when I
went yesterday to see what the dear little creatures
were doing, the marten had taken the nest away
from me and not a piece of it was left. And now,
no matter where I go, I can think of nothing but
my loss. Indeed, who can tell about the water of
forgetfulness! But do you know something, dear
fellow? Just go to the old woman of the forest,
who is wiser than other people and perhaps knows
the fountain of forgetfulness." Thereupon the raven told the huntsman the way to the old woman
of the forest. Heinz thanked him, and went on.

The old woman was at home. She sat in front
of her cottage, spinning, and nodding her white
head. By her side a gray cat, with grass-green
eyes, sat licking her paws and purring.

Heinz stepped up to the old woman, greeted her
respectfully, and made known his errand.

"I know everything about the fountain of forgetfulness," said the old woman of the forest,
"and will not withhold a drink of its waters from
you, poor boy. But no work, no pay: if you wish
to have a glass of the precious drink, you must
first perform three tasks for me. Will you do
it?"

"If I can."

"I do not expect impossibilities of you. To begin with, you shall cut down the wood behind my house. That is the first labor."

The young fellow consented. The old woman gave him an axe and led him to the place. Heinz stretched himself and swung the axe, and every time he struck a blow he imagined that he hit his rival, and the trees fell crashing beneath his mighty strokes, and the crashing did him good. Thus evening came on, and Heinz looked about for food, for he was very hungry. He did not have long to wait, for out of the house came a woman's figure, who placed a basket with food and drink beside the weary wood-cutter.

As Heinz raised his eyes, he saw before him a wonderfully lovely face, framed in yellow hair, on which gleamed the last rays of the setting sun. It was the old forest woman's daughter. She looked at the sad young fellow with gentle eyes, and remained standing before him awhile. But as he said nothing, she went away again. Heinz ate and drank. Then he gathered together fir boughs and wood moss for a bed, laid himself down, and slept a dreamless sleep. But when he awoke in the morning, his sorrow awoke again too.

Then he seized the axe and attacked the trees, so

that the forest, for a mile around, resounded with
his mighty blows.   And when at evening the
beautiful maiden came with his supper, Heinz
did not look as sad as the day before; and because he felt that he must say something, he said,
"Fine weather to-day." Whereupon the maiden
answered, "Yes, very fine weather," and then
nodded and went home.

Thus seven days passed away, each one like the
other, and on the seventh day the last tree was
cut down.   The old forest woman came out,
praised Heinz for his industry, and said, "Now
comes the second task."

Then Heinz had to dig up the roots of the trees,
break up the soil, plant corn, and sow seed.   This
took him seven weeks.   But every evening, after
his day's work was done, the old woman's daughter brought him his supper and sat near by on the
trunk of a tree, and listened to Heinz as he told
her about the outside world, and when he finished
she gave him her white hand and said, "Good
night, dear Heinz."   Then she went home, but
Heinz looked about for a resting place and immediately fell asleep.

When the seven weeks were gone, the old woman came and looked at his work, praised the

youth for his industry, and said: "Now comes the
third task. Now with the wood you have felled
you must build me a house with seven rooms, and
when you have finished that too, then you shall
have a glass of the water of forgetfulness, and can
go wherever you please."

Then Heinz became a carpenter, and with axe
and saw he built a splendid house. To be sure,
the work went on slowly at first, because Heinz
worked without help; but that was not distasteful
to him, for he enjoyed the green forest, and would
have liked to live always near the old woman. Indeed, he sometimes thought still of his former
sorrow, but only as one who has had a bad dream,
and in the morning is glad that he has awakened
from it. Every evening the forest woman's daughter came out to him, and they sang together,
sometimes gay hunting songs, sometimes songs
which told of parting, of unrequited love and joyful meetings.

Thus seven months passed by. Then the house
was finished from threshold to roof-tree. Heinz
had placed a young fir-tree on the gable, and the
maiden had made wreaths of fir-twigs and red
berries from the mountain-ash, and trimmed the
walls with them. The old woman came on her

crutch, with the cat on her shoulder, to inspect the completed work. She looked very solemn, and in her hand she carried a goblet carved out of wood, and filled with the water of forgetfulness.

"You have performed the three tasks which I have imposed upon you," she said, "and now comes the reward. Take this goblet, and when you have emptied it to the last drop, then the past will be blotted out of your memory."

The forester hesitated as he reached out his hand towards the goblet.

"Drink," said the old woman, "and forget everything."

"Everything?"

"Yes, everything — your former sorrow, myself, and — "

"And me, too," said the beautiful maiden, and she held her hand before her eyes to keep back the rising tears.

Then the youth seized the goblet and with his strong hand flung it on the ground, so that the sparkling drops of the water rained down on the grass, and he cried, "Mother, I will stay with you!"

And before he knew what had happened to him, the maiden lay on his breast and sobbed for joy.

And a rustling went through the trees, and the yellow corn all around nodded in the wind, the birds sang in the branches, and the old woman's gray cat went purring round and round the happy pair.

Now I could without much difficulty change the old woman into a beautiful fairy, her daughter to a princess, and the newly built house to a shining royal castle; but let us rather keep to the truth, and let everything be as it was.

But something wonderful really did happen. Wherever a drop of the water of forgetfulness fell on the ground, there sprang up a little flower with eyes of heavenly blue. The flower has since spread over the whole land, and for those who do not know its name this story was not written.

THEODELINDA
AND THE WATER-SPRITE.

ON the edge of the forest, where the flowers
grow that do not thrive in the deeper shade,
where the brown field-mice dwell and the green
lizards, where the wren dodges through the bushes
and beetles in golden coats of mail tumble about
the wild roses, there stood, like sentinels, two primeval pine-trees, which seemed to grow from the
same root. At the foot of the twin trees was a
seat formed of stones and moss, and on the seat
sat a lady who only differed from the majority of
her sisters in that her form showed hollows, where
one was usually accustomed to find roundness.
She wore a sky-blue dress and a broad-brimmed
straw hat, which shaded a yellowish face, framed
by two bread-colored curls. In her right hand she
held a dainty pencil, in her left a little red book,
on the cover of which, in gold letters, was in-
scribed these words: "The Blossoms of Theodelinda's Mind."

Theodelinda was a poetess, and the latest blossom of her mind ran thus : —

> In cool moss by the wood
> A lovely rose-bush stood.
> There came a lad one day
> And broke a rose away.
>
> The rose, in sorrow, said,
> " He will my petals shed;
> Yet sweet it is to die,
> If on his breast I lie."

The verses were written down, and the poetess' watery blue eyes looked longingly into the distance, but the lad of whom she was thinking would not come; the lad was at that moment sitting with two boisterous companions, drinking, in the forest tavern of the White Stag, and never dreamed of breaking the little rose.

Theodelinda sighed, and picked a daisy which was growing in the grass at her feet. " He loves me," she murmured, as her sharp fingers pulled off the white petals, — " he loves me with all his heart — passionately — beyond measure — desperately — a little — not at all." Alas, poor Theodelinda!

"That is absurd child's play," she said, and threw the mutilated flower contemptuously on the ground. Then she tucked up her dress and walked away into the woods, probably to pluck one or two more of the blossoms of her mind in its sacred dim shade.

If Theodelinda had not been a city girl, but a peasant child of the mountains, she would have been much more careful when she undertook to go through the woods; and, above all things, would have put in her shoe a little branch of the shrub which renders harmless all magic charms. Then what came to pass would hardly have happened to her. But what could a poor city lass know about the secrets of the forest?

Where the mightiest fir-trees, with long gray beards of moss stand, in the shade grows a plant called "err-wort." Nobody except the woodpecker, who knows all magic plants, has ever seen it, but many a one who has stepped on it unawares, and not had the counter-charm with him, must have felt its effect.

While the poetess was trying to add "love" and "dove" "heart" and "part" to the blossoms of her thought, she went gradually deeper and

deeper into the forest. The approaching twilight
and a longing in the region of the stomach,
which ordinary mortals call hunger, first warned
the pleasure-seeker that it was time to return
home. She turned to go back by the way she
had come, but it seemed to her as though the
forest were endless, for she went around in a
circle, and the err-wort, on which she had stepped
unawares, was to blame for it. Oh, misery! oh,
misery! It grew darker and darker all the time.
The shadowy creatures of the night glided across
the path, and the hooting of the robber owls
was heard. Theodelinda was in despair.

Suddenly she found herself before a little
house, out of whose window shone a faint light.
With thankful heart she knocked on the door;
it opened, and she went in.

In the hut were three trim little women, no
larger than half-grown girls, busy baking cakes
on the hearth. They were little forest folk.
They are usually invisible, but whoever steps
on the err-wort is able to see the little forest
folk, and many other things besides.

They received the wanderer with kindness
and attention, pushed a stool up to the fire for
her, and entertained her with bread and milk.

Theodelinda felt confidence in them, and was soon quite at her ease in their company, for they promised when the morning came to show her the right way.

"This is for once a real adventure, such as only a poet can meet with," thought Theodelinda; and she experienced the feeling of gentle horror, mingled with satisfaction, of a child listening to a ghost story. But it was going to be still better.

Suddenly there was a tapping on the window, and a man's voice was heard to say : —

> "Open the door, ye sisters dear!
> The moon shines on the waters clear.
> It led me through the forest way.
> Open the door, good sisters, pray!"

"There he is again," said one of the little women ; "the fiend, the nuisance ! his mother, the old nixie, sends him here. She wants him to marry, so that the thoughtless fellow may become orderly and domestic, and so she thinks that one of us ought to count it an honor to become her daughter-in-law. But I would rather be a spinster than leave my green forest and become his wife."

"And so would I !" "And so would I !" said the

other two little women. But Theodelinda said
not a word.

"We must let him in," continued the first
one; "that can do no harm. He is a very
dangerous fellow, and we dare not arouse his
anger." And, with a sigh, she unbolted the door.

The water-sprite came in. He had a pretty
face and a slender form. To be sure, he had
green hair, but Miss Theodelinda thought it
was very becoming to him.

The guest looked somewhat disturbed when
he discovered what a visitor the little folk had,
but, like a well-bred person, he did not allow
his displeasure to be noticed, and made himself as charming as only a water-sprite knows
how to be.

Theodelinda was very talkative; she told
about balls and the theatre, and the water-
sprite listened patiently. Then he had to tell
something about himself, and he did it graciously.

Indeed, he was a fine man, and probably much
better than his reputation. And besides, he had
a crystal castle in the lake, which was not to be
despised, and the old mother nixie was surely a
very fine woman. Thus thought Theodelinda;
and in her mind she was already rocking on the

waves like Melusina, and floating through the air in a feathery robe.

She longed to make an impression on the water-sprite. Therefore, after a few preliminary remarks, she took the little red book out of her bosom and began to read her poetry.

For some time the water-sprite listened and murmured words of appreciation. But suddenly he jumped up and exclaimed: "Gracious goodness! I had almost forgotten that I was invited by the wild huntsman and Lady Holle to a card party. I beg you to excuse me." Having spoken these words, he rushed out of the house.

Theodelinda looked out, surprised, at the door through which he had fled. But the little forest people clapped their hands and cried joyfully: "You have done well; you have done well! You must have a present as a reward."

And one of the little women went to a chest, took a skein of blue yarn out of it, and handed it to the poetess with these words: "Take good care of it; there is a blessing with it."

Theodelinda did not know what to make of it all.

Vexed at the behavior of the water-sprite, and tired from the day's exertion, she begged her to

show her to a sleeping-place. The little women
heaped up a bed of leaves for her. Then she lay
down and fell asleep.

When she awoke, she was lying on the edge
of the wood, under the twin pines. The cool
morning wind was blowing through the tops of
the trees and playing with Theodelinda's bread-
colored locks.

"So I have been dreaming," she said to herself, "and slept all night in the woods." She
felt in the place where she was accustomed to
put away her red book, but the book was gone.
She jumped up in alarm, and then a great skein
of blue yarn rolled out of her lap on the ground.
So it wasn't a dream, after all.

She hunted for her red book, but it had disappeared forever. Chilly, and out of sorts, she
tried to reach home as soon as possible, to recover
from her adventure in the forest. It ended in a
hard cold.

While Theodelinda was shut up in her room
on account of her indisposition, she wrote her
poetry from memory in a new book. The little
forest women had taken the old one away from
her, while she slept, in order to use the blossoms
of Theodelinda's mind as effectual weapons

against the water-sprite's obtrusiveness. Indeed, that put an end to his visits, and soon after he married the daughter of a nixie of good family.

But the blue skein of yarn which the little forest folk had given the poetess as a present, was no ordinary skein; unwind as much of it as you pleased, you would never come to the end.

And Miss Theodelinda knit stocking after stocking, and made verses at the same time; and when she went along the street, the people said, "Here comes the blue-stocking."

THE ASS'S SPRING.

IN a green valley, shut in by steep heights, a cool, abundant spring, called the Ass's Well, has its source. The spring is inclosed, and covered over with a canopy, on the top of which turns a tin ass as weather vane.

Every morning in summer there stand by the edge of the well, pale young ladies from the city, who, under the care of anxious mothers and protecting aunts, drink the cold water from handsome mugs. City gentlemen, too, visit the spring, and indeed not only the sickly ones, but also healthy youths with brown faces, and bold-twisted mustaches. A warrior, gray with age, who for thirty years had come and gone with the swallows; a poetical, incomprehensible young lady, with long, straw-colored curls; a mysterious widow in deep mourning; a prestigiator, who is especially sought after in rainy weather, and who makes money vanish and guesses drawn cards; — all these characters are to be found at the ass's well, and therefore there is no lack of what belongs to a so-called " summer resort." But wait! we had almost forgotten the most important feature, the landlady of the *Golden Goose*. She rules with unlimited power, cooks well, and treats high and low with an honest brusqueness which to the city people is as refreshing as May dew.

There is great difference of opinion about the origin of the name the well bears. Some say that a thirsty ass disclosed the spring by pawing with his hoofs. Others claim that the well is so called because its waters, like ass's milk, are beneficial to feeble constitutions. But both opinions are at fault. This will become clear as daylight to all who read this story to the end.

Many, many years ago, when the mightiest tree in the forest was still a germ sleeping in a brown acorn, nothing was known of the healing power of the future Ass's Well. The visitors who came to its brink were the beasts of the forest or grazing cattle, and deer; wood-cutters, huntsmen and char-coal-burners; and men praised the cool water, and the beasts did the same after their own fashion.

One day two stood by the well, — one on this

side, the other on that. He was an ass, and she was a goose, both in the first bloom of youth. They greeted each other silently, and quenched their thirst. Then the ass drew near to the goose, and asked bashfully, "Young lady, may I accompany you?"

She nodded, and would gladly have blushed, but this she was unable to do, and they went together through the meadow and talked about the weather. They had gone quite a distance, when the ass stood still and asked, "Young lady, whither does your way lead?"

The goose looked sadly at her companion askance, and said quietly, "How do I know? Oh, I am the most unfortunate creature under the sun!" And as the ass questioned her further, and urged her to pour out her heart, she related the story of her life.

"I am called Alheid," said the goose, "and am of good family. My ancestor was one of the sacred geese that saved the capital. You know the story, young gentleman?"

The ass said hesitatingly, "Ye-es." He had really never heard of the story, but he did not wish to grieve the goose.

"Another of my maternal ancestors," continued

Alheid, " was on friendly terms with Saint Martin
She is said, according to the sad legend, to have
given her life for him. But I will not dwell on
the history of my ancestors, but tell you about
myself. I came to the light of the world, together
with eleven brothers and sisters, and, indeed, on
a farm, where my mother as a brooding goose
lived a life appropriate to her station. I was
my mother's pet, for in our family the youngest
child is always the most talented."

"Just as it is in ours," remarked the ass.

"I will pass over the years of my childhood,"
continued the goose, "the happy plays in the
village pond and in the lake of the castle garden,
where, in the company of the young swans, I
acquired that elegance of motion for which I have
been so often admired. I had long before shed
the yellow down of youth and had blossomed into
the prime of life. Then, one day there appeared
on the farm a man, who had a very hooked nose;
his temples were adorned on the right and on
the left with two shiny black curls, and over his
shoulder hung a pack. The farmer's wife and
the maids flocked around him, and looked with
longing eyes at the bright-colored ribbons and
cloths which he took out of his bag. To make

a long story short, I was caught, and with my feet and wings bound I was given over to the stranger, who took me in exchange for a blue handkerchief decorated with red roses. Now came melancholy days. I was shut up in a narrow coop, and given balls of barley flour to fatten me. With horror I noticed that my circumference increased from day to day, and even my grief over my wretched plight was unable to arrest the evil."

Here the ass cast a look at his companion's figure, and swore that he never had seen a more elegant goose. With a look of thankfulness at the ass, Alheid continued : —

"Last night — I shudder to think of it — I heard woful cries of agony, which evidently came from the throat of one of my fellow-prisoners. I saw two eyes shine in the moonlight, and heard the death-rattle. A fox or a polecat must have broken into the coop. Fear lent me strength. I forced myself through the bars of my prison and escaped. I was saved. My wings bore me to this valley; and now I shall try to prolong my life as a wild goose, until winter comes, when I shall, perhaps, find a modest position as snow goose."

Alheid sighed deeply, and then was silent.

"My fate," said the ass, "is similar to yours, Miss Alheid. Look at the black cross which decorates my shoulder; that will tell you all. I am of the race of the sacred ass of Jerusalem, and Baldwin is my name. My pedigree goes back to Noah's ark. Balaam's ass, and the ass with whose jawbone Samson slew two thousand Philistines are my ancestors. The one of my ancestors who died like a philosopher between two bundles of hay, I will only mention incidently; nor will I dwell on the worthiest of my high-aspiring fore-fathers, who founded the collateral branch of mules. My parents were convent people, and bore pious monks on their errands of charity. My older brothers and sisters became lay brethren; but the fathers sold me to the convent miller, and I, a sacred ass, saw myself compelled by rough men to carry contemptible meal sacks. For a long time I suffered in silent submission. But one night, when the cruelty of a rough miller's boy drove me to desperation, I burst my fetters, and came to this peaceful forest valley, where I found you by the cool well, most charming Alheid. Here I think I shall remain for the present, and lead the contemplative life of a wild ass."

So the ass and the goose both remained in the meadow valley. They dwelt apart from each other, as it became them, but they saw each other and talked together daily, and at last one could no longer live without the other. They were happy and sad at the same time; happy, because they loved and found love in return; sad, because they saw that they could never belong to one another.

"Oh! why was I born a goose!" bewailed Alheid; and Baldwin, the ass, sighed, "If I were a bird!" and he knew, too, what kind of a bird he would be.

Thus weeks passed by. The ass grew perceptibly thin, although there was no lack of nourishing food in the meadow valley; and the goose lost the red color from her bill, and her eyes became dull.

Now, there lived in the forest, in a hollow stone, an owl, who was the most clever female anywhere about, and the beasts often went to her for advice. The ass told her his distress, and when the owl had heard his story, she said: "That I cannot help. But wait till Midsummer. Then the wise Wish-Lady comes to the well in the meadow valley to bathe. Confide to her your trouble. Perhaps she will help you, and change your form; she is a powerful magician."

Then the ass went away half consoled. On Midsummer eve, when Alheid, the goose, had sought her resting-place, he concealed himself near the spring to wait for the Wish-Lady.

She did not keep him waiting long. She came flying along in her dress of swan's feathers, threw aside the downy garment, and bathed her white limbs in the cool spring. The ass waited with an ass's patience until she came out of the water; and when she had sat down on a stone and was combing her hair, then Baldwin stepped up to her, beat his fore-hoof three times as a greeting, and begged the Wish-Lady, piteously, to change him to a gander.

The enchantress shook her head. "That is a strange wish," she thought, "but I can fulfil it and I will."

And she whispered in the ear of the ass, who listened attentively: "Early to-morrow morning, at sunrise, pick seven goose-berry blossoms [1] and eat them silently, then plunge your head in the well, and you will be changed to a fine gander. And now go your way, and leave me alone."

[1] In the German *gänse-blume* (literally goose-flower), the ox-eyed daisy.

The ass thanked her heartily, and went away. He never closed his eyes all night, and as soon as the mountain-tops began to grow red, he was up on his feet and away to look for the seven goose-berry blossoms. Then he hurried to the spring, and plunged his head in, and when he drew it out again, to his delight, he saw in the mirror of the water the picture of a handsome gander with a beautifully curved neck.

As fast as he could go, he hurried to the thicket where the goose had taken up her abode. "Alheid, my beloved Alheid!" he cried, "where art thou?"

"Here, my dearest, sounded from the thicket, and a pretty little she-ass came dancing out of the bushes.

The lovers looked at each other, dumb with amazement.

"Oh, what an ass I am!" sighed the gander.

"Oh, what a goose I am!" groaned the ass.

Then a hot torrent of tears poured from their eyes; and in the midst of her weeping Alheid told how she had followed the advice of the owl, and sought the Wish-Lady, who had granted her request, and changed her to a jenny. Hereupon the gander, between heavy sobs, gave his experience, and the Midsummer sun never shone on two more wretched creatures than our two lovers.

Time heals all things. Calm endurance took the place of uncontrollable anguish. One hope was left to the pair. Perhaps the Wish-Lady, on her next visit to the spring, would restore one of the lovers to the original form. But before that a whole year must pass. Patience, then, patience! So Baldwin and Alheid again lived together like brother and sister.

After much distress and danger, which the winter brought to the two anchorites, spring appeared in the land; the sun mounted higher and higher, and at last Midsummer eve had come.

With beating hearts the lovers this time went together to the well, and stated their case to the Wish-Lady.

"This is a bad affair," said the enchantress. "I cannot change either of you back again, however willing I may be to grant you the favor. But I will make you a proposition. How would it do if you became human beings? Out of an ass and a goose it would not be difficult to make a youth and a maiden: that I can do. Would that please you?"

"Yes," cried Baldwin and Alheid with one voice.

The Wish-Lady murmured a charm, and told them both to plunge their heads in the well. They obeyed, and when they took them out again Baldwin had became a sturdy young man with an extremely good-natured face, and opposite him stood a charming little woman with a prettily arched, rosy mouth, and languishing eyes.

And they fell down at the Wish-Lady's feet and gratefully kissed her hands, and then they kissed each others' lips and whispered words of love in each others' ears. But the Wish-Lady, noticing that her presence was superfluous, wrapped herself in her dress of feathers and flew away.

The two young people remained in the meadow valley. Baldwin built a house, and in it they passed a happy life; and each year a little child was given them, sometimes a boy and sometimes a girl.

In the neighboring villages nobody suspected that Baldwin had been an ass, and Alheid a goose, for they were as sensible as other human beings. They did not make a great noise about the history of their transformation, as it would have prejudiced them in the eyes of the people. But when they were about to die they intrusted it as a secret to their eldest son, and it was he who named the house "The Golden Goose," and the spring "The Ass's Well," as they are still called at the present day.

How the healing power of the waters was discovered, and how life gradually came to the remote forest valley, are very fully described in a book which the landlady sells to the guests who use the waters.

The Wish-Lady has for a long time stayed away, probably because it is too noisy for her in the valley. But even at the present time it happens that almost every year some young pair is seen at the spring, who seem as well adapted to each other as the heroes of our story.

THE TALKATIVE HOUSE–KEY.

———•◦•———

THIS is what happens when one spends his
whole summer spinning yarns and meddles
with kobolds, nixies, and beasts that talk.

A sedate man who restrains his fancy judiciously could never have met with the adventure
which I experienced the other day, and will relate
as follows : —

I had returned to the city from my summer
vacation, and had already spent two or three days
wandering about the streets in search of a dwell-
ing-place suited to my needs. For urgent reasons
I did not make the most splendid quarter the
province of my research, but that part of the city
in whose narrow alleys the so-called poor people
fight the battle of existence. Why the street in
which I at last found what I was looking for
was called Heaven's Gate I have not been able
to discover. Towards the east it ran into Butcher
Street, where bloody calves and pale pigs hung

from iron hooks, and towards the west the Gate
led into the so-called Jews' Square, which was no
paradise either.

My attention was drawn to a little pasteboard
card fastened to an arched door which was
painted green. "Furnished room in the fourth
story, to let to a single gentleman," it said. I
looked at the house. It had been freshly painted;
and behind the windows could be seen white cur-
tains and red pinks. The door was decorated
with two brass lions' heads, which looked as
amiable as two serene poodles; and above the door
the metal number of the house — 9 — the number
of the muses, — greeted my eyes. I rang the bell.

An elderly woman, neatly attired, opened the
door, asked courteously what I wished, and when I
had told her my errand, took me up four dark and
rather steep flights of stairs to inspect the room
which was to let. Having reached the top, she
opened the door and let me step into the room.
It was what I needed, — a small room, clean and
airy, and high above the dampness and noise of
the street, with an outlook on a maze of roofs,
over which wandered a variety of cats with their
elegant gait; above, the gleaming chimney swallows sailed through the blue air, and in the distance was the reticulated spire of the cathedral.

The rent was soon agreed upon, and through our mutual representations I learned that my present landlady herself was no less than the owner of the house, and the wife of a shoemaker, who worked on the first floor. I took my luggage from the hotel, and an hour later I was on the point of settling myself comfortably in my new quarters. My effects were soon unpacked and disposed of. The one table which the room contained was appropriated as a writing-desk and placed near the window. The inkstand was freshly filled, and everything was in order.

"Now, Lady Muse, you may pay me a visit as soon as you wish!" I cried out. Then the door opened; but it was not the muse who entered, but the lady of the house.

"I had almost forgotten it," she said, laughing, and held the latch-key towards me. She wiped it carefully on her apron, although it was of polished steel, looked at it almost tenderly, and handed it to me. "If it could talk!" she added, and then I was alone with the latch-key.

It was a strong old fellow. But no! that is not the proper expression; it had rather the appearance of a worthy patriarch; its ward was carefully hollowed out, and the handle was so large that one could put his whole hand through it. I allotted the key its place on a nail, and sat down to write, to inform those persons who took an interest in me of my present place of abode.

A week later I was, so to speak, in the traces; my day's work was laid out. The morning I spent at the city library, the larger part of the rest of the day in my watch-tower at No. 9 Heaven's Gate. I should have liked to pass my evenings at the *Green Hedgehog*, where, according to the report of several reliable gentlemen, whose acquaintance I had made, an excellent native wine was on draught; but the cruelly low state of my finances confined me to my tea-urn, which my landlady filled with water every evening, and kept very bright and clean.

The first of the next month brought me a modest income; and, as soon as it grew dark, I took the house-key with me, and with a look of disdain at the tea-urn left the house to seek the *Green Hedgehog*. The wine was really not bad, and the conversation as good as it can be only in a circle of young men who are trying to forget in a strong drink the burden and care of the day, and the rebuke of the night before.

I came home in high spirits, and rather late,
and considering my cheerful frame of mind, nobody would think it strange that while I was
undressing I sang the old student's song:

"At my lodgings I've studied the whole forenoon."

Then all of a sudden it seemed to me as if
a deep bass voice joined in my song, and when
I looked around in alarm, I saw to my greatest
amazement that my house-key was swinging on
its nail like a pendulum, and I distinctly heard
it humming, "I'll not stir an inch from this
place till the watchman cries *twelve* in my face. —
Juvivallerala!"

I stood still in astonishment. Nothing like
it had ever happened to me before.

"House-key, old fellow," I cried, "what is the
matter with you?"

"I have no objection," answered the house-
key, "to your familiarity, although you are only
a lodger, and not the owner of the house; but
if you address me so, then you must allow me
the same privilege."

"Willingly; but tell me first of all —"

"How I came to have the power of speech?
That I will tell you by and by, for I hope we
shall be together a long time yet. So in the

mean time accept the fact as it is and do not
rack your brains unnecessarily about it. In the
next place, accept my thanks for having taken
me with you to the tavern. You cannot believe
how much good it does an old house-key, who
has not crossed his own threshold for a whole
year, to breathe once more the air of an inn."

Here the key began to swing like a pendulum
again, and hummed at the same time, "Straight
from the tavern I am coming."

I could not yet become accustomed to the
miracle, and for the sake of saying something,
I said, "You seem to be well versed in drinking-
songs."

"So I think," answered the key. "Shall I
perhaps sing you a 'Gaudeamus igitur,' or, 'The
professor gives no lecture to-day'?"

"Let it be till another time. Singing might
wake up the neighbors."

"Very well," continued the talkative house-
key, "then we will chat together. You are not
sleepy yet? Shall I tell you to whom I am in-
debted for all my merry drinking-songs? Oh,
those were fine times!"

The house-key paused as if he were rumma-
ging in the bottom of his memory.

"I propose," he then continued, "that you lie down and put out the light. I can tell the story better in the dark."

And I did as he wished.

"I have never seen a handsomer youth," began the narrator, "than the one I am now going to tell you about. Everybody liked him, and so did I, although through him I have often been placed in a very awkward position. At that time he was a boy of about ten years, and looked roguishly out of a pair of large brown eyes. I was in the service of his parents, but had not yet come in contact with the merry Willie. So I was all the more delighted when the little fellow took me down one day from the nail, put me in his pocket and carried me out-doors. When we reached the city park he took me out and showed me to some boys who were his play-fellows. The oldest one turned me over and over, looked into my mouth, and pronounced me fit to be used. For what purpose I learned soon enough. The boy took a file out of his pocket and began to rasp me, so that sight and hearing left me. When he had made a deep wound in me, he poured a black powder inside me and placed a wad of paper on top."

"Aha!" said I, interrupting the narrator, "so you became a key-pistol."

"Yes, a key-pistol. I, the house-key of house No. 9 Heaven's Gate. But, —

> His days indeed are wisely spent,
> Who with his station is content;

and I determined to do honor to mine. Without trembling I awaited the burning slow-match, and — crack! — flew the charge out of my mouth, so that the sparrows in the park flew off, seized with sudden fright.

"The crowd of boys too fled in alarm, but the cause of their sudden fright was not myself, but a man, who wore a blue coat with brass buttons, and on his white belt a sword. Unnoticed he had emerged from behind the elder-bushes, and with the cry, 'I've got you, you rascals!' he made a dash at the boys. To be sure, he didn't get near them, for they had already reached a place of safety, but I, the innocent one, was seized and taken away.

"'Farewell, No. 9 Heaven's Gate,' I sighed; and in my mind I already saw myself amongst old iron, in the company of bent nails and rusty stove-doors. But it was to be otherwise. As soon as

Willie's father missed me, he began to search for me everywhere, and the one who alone could give information of my whereabouts judiciously held his peace; so the anxious man, fearing that I might have been taken for criminal purposes, immediately went to the police, to report the case.

"The joy which I felt when the police officer, with a mild smile, asked my master if I were the missing key, and the face Willie's father made when he learned how I had come into the hands of the police, I am unable to describe in words. I was returned to my rightful owner, and carried home in his coat pocket, after he had paid a dollar as a fine for forbidden shooting within the city limits. The unpleasant scene between father and son, which concluded the adventure, I will pass over in silence. The wound which the boys gave me, when they made a key-pistol out of me, was healed by a locksmith. If you examine me carefully to-morrow, you will detect, an inch above my handle, a reddish scar. I am not ashamed of it."

The house-key paused a moment, as if to get his breath, and then continued:—

"My friend Willie now seemed to avoid me

studiously. At first, after the occurrence I have
just told you of, he looked at me slyly, and then
he ceased to look at me at all. Thus passed
several years. Willie had become a handsome,
slender youth, and his mother told him so every
day. He already had a tobacco-pipe with bright-
colored tassels, and he filled it from his father's
tobacco pouch when his father's back was turned.
Sometimes he came home late in the evening with
a heated brain, and then his father would scold,
and his mother had great difficulty in defending
her son.

"One evening Willie stayed out excessively late,
and his father stormed worse than ever. 'I'll let
the young scapegrace see how he gets into the
house,' said he, finally, in great anger, and he
locked the front door himself, laid me under his
pillow, and went to sleep. But his mother was
awake. She cautiously drew me out from beneath
the bolster, and tied me up carefully in a handkerchief. Then she placed herself by the window to
wait, and when about midnight Willie came creep-
ing along, she dropped me down on the street.
Her son seized me, and after fumbling about some
time for the key-hole, opened the door, and when
he had given me back to his anxious mother,

groped his way along to his chamber. How his father was pacified the next morning I do not remember.

"Again some time passed by, and then came a festal day. The father himself gave me over to his son, — who was now called a student and wore a red cap, — and made a long speech, which he ended by saying that Willie must always show himself worthy of me. The son thanked him with emotion and received me with beaming eyes. I once heard that the king bestows golden keys upon people of high rank, and that this is a great honor; but I can hardly believe that one of them ever experienced so great joy at this distinction as my Willie felt when he put me in his pocket.

"The day when the key was given over was followed by the merriest night which I ever spent, and it will live in my memory till I have crumbled away to rust. He who was now my owner carried me to the rooms of the club of which he was to become a member. Ah, then there was a high old time! Gay carousers with bright-colored caps and belts, waiting-maids with white aprons and black eyes, full mugs and drinking-horns, shining rapiers, merry songs, jollity and noise till morning light."

"I know all about that, house-key. I know all about that."

"The merriest of them all was my Willie. He was so delighted at having possession of me that he gave his companions a keg of the best beer; and the knowledge that, as owner of a house-key, he was admitted to the circle of free and independent men, made him very bold towards the brown-haired Toni. When Willie reached Heaven's Gate the sun was already up, and the door of house No. 9 had just been unfastened. The first time that I was at Willie's disposal he had no need of me.

"Now began the merriest time of my life. Many similar evenings followed this first one like the beads of a rosary. In the mean time there were drives, torchlight processions, drinking-parties, and many merry college tricks; and I was always present, for the advice of the philosopher,

> The crafty tippler his house-key takes
> At early morn when he awakes,

was wisely followed by my master. Moreover, that as academical house-key I did not let the time pass unemployed I have already given you proof.

"Under the circumstances, my share in the
events of my master's life was a passive one. Oh,
if I had never left the roll of a spectator! That
unfortunate moment when I became active in the
course of events was the cause of everlasting
separation from my Willie. I will be brief, for
the pain of recollection forbids me any flowers of
speech. Besides, it is late in the night, and you
will want to go to sleep.

"My friend Willie had gone with his companions
to a village, and there the young men were having
a good time over their glasses, laughing, shouting,
and singing. But not far from the table where
the students were drinking, a crowd of journey-
men mechanics, rough, but strong men, had sat
down.

"I do not know whether it is now as it was then.
At that time, whenever students and mechanics,
whom we collegians called 'snags,' met, they began
to banter each other. But this time it soon grew
into a quarrel, and it was my master who, by singing the song 'God bless you, brother bristler,'
commenced hostilities. At first, insulting words
passed back and forth; later on, beer mugs, and
other things that happened to be at hand; and
when these missiles gave out, they seized sticks

and the legs of chairs. How the unlucky thought
of using me as a weapon came into my owner's head,
I do not know; I only know that I did great mischief in the young fellow's hand. But let us draw
the curtain over this unprofitable scene.

"After that day I found myself once more in
the hands of justice, and had a fine Latin name
given to me, which has escaped my memory."

" Probably it was *corpus delicti*, was it not?"

"Quite right!" cried the house-key with delight. " As *corpus delicti* I was put with the
reports, but my poor young friend sat in a narrow
room, whose doors were bolted outside and the
windows furnished with iron gratings. People
call it a prison."

" I know all about that, too, house-key.

" So much the better, as it will save me from
going into details. But give me your attention a
few minutes longer. I am almost at the end. The
affair in which we were concerned turned out
very badly. Willie was expelled; and when he
had paid his fine, left the city. To be sure, I
went back to my home; but my merry life was
all over. Sad at heart, I spent my days on a nail
in a dark corner; and what I learned from time
to time about my darling from his parents' con-

versation did not help to lessen my sadness.
Trouble gnawed at the hearts of the two old
people and rust gnawed at mine. It was a lucky
day for me that a change soon took place in my
circumstances. Willie's parents sold the house —
it was said, to pay their son's debts — and I passed
into other hands, — hands which cleaned away
the rust from me, and by repeated oilings restored
my lost virtues.

"I have never heard a word about Willie's parents; but himself I have seen once since then,
and this meeting I will tell you about to-morrow.
For the present, good night."

" Good night, house-key ! "

On the following morning, when I awoke
somewhat later than usual, my house-key was
hanging silently on its nail, and to my faint-
hearted " good morning " gave no reply. " Probably," I thought, " he speaks only at midnight; or,
still more probably, it was all a dream." The
last supposition seemed to me more and more
likely, in proportion as sleep left my limbs.
" How can one dream such foolish stuff ! " I
said to myself; " the home-made wine and the
gay conversation of last evening were to blame
for it." I dressed myself and went to my daily

work, which, like yesterday, I crowned with a
visit to the *Green Hedgehog.*

"Now we shall soon see whether I was dreaming or not," I said, as I returned to my room
towards midnight. "How are you, old house-
key?"

"Thank you for the kind inquiry; very well,"
sounded the answer. "I am always feeling
well when I have breathed the fragrance of
wine."

So it was a fact, and no dream. I opened
the window and put my head out. A falling
star made a bright arch in the sky, and across
from the cathedral sounded the striking of
bells. I pulled my ear. No, I was not dreaming. I really possessed a talking house-key.

"May I talk with you again a little while?"
he asked courteously.

"Nothing would please me better," I replied,
politely put out the light, and stretched myself
at full length on my bed.

"About two years after the event I last described," began the key, "I was in the service
of a man who had this very room which you
now occupy, and who, like you, lived by writing.
He was not very old then, but his thin hair

was already turning gray, and gray was also
the color of his wrinkled face. It seemed to be
his favorite color, for he usually wore gray
clothes too, and even gray spectacles; gray dust
lay on his books, and gray ink flowed from his pen
on grayish paper.

"This man possessed the faculty of seeing the
imperfections of anything at the first glance.
When he took me for the first time in his hand
he immediately spied the scar which I carry as
a remembrance of the time when I served as a
key-pistol. 'Patched!' he said, with a spiteful
laugh, and pushed me away from him. When
the morning sun looked in at the window to
greet him, he spoke of sun-spots; when the moon
rose in the evening above the gabled roof, he
would say, 'She has neither air nor water'; and
if he went out into the park in May-time, he
did not see the young leaves and the white blossoms, but only the caterpillars on them.

"There was a good reason for the gray man's
bitter manners. He had made a compact with
Gallus, the ink-devil, who all day long sat in a
great dust-covered inkstand and came out at
night to squat on the paper-weight and help
his master write. But the suggestions of a

wicked ink-devil are not as sweet as honey.
The gray man was a so-called critic. Do you
know what that is?"

"I know what it is; go on, house-key, go
on!"

"My owner seldom made use of me. The
crabbed man never went into gay company,
therefore he often visited the theatre, and then
he took me with him, so I am under some
obligation to him for enlarging my knowledge.
To be sure, he seldom remained long, but usually
left the house soon after the first act, which in
no way prevented him from criticising the rest.

"One evening he took me — as it seemed to me,
with an uncanny laugh — from the nail, examined
my mouth, put me in his pocket, and went out
of the house. By the direction which we took,
and the length of the way, I concluded that the
gray man was going to a theatre in the suburbs;
and so he was. He went in and took a seat. They
were tuning the instruments in the orchestra; the
doors of the boxes slammed; a humming sound
gave reason to conclude that the house was filling up; the music began; the curtain rose, and
the play commenced. I could only follow it in-
telligently with my ears, for my seat was in

my master's dark coat pocket, and the opera
glass, which repelled all my attempts to get
nearer with haughty silence, was often the object of my envy. To-day the play was to be a
play for me in the true sense of the word, for
my master took me out of my dark dungeon
and allowed me a look at the audience and the
stage.

"Saint Florian! what did I see! On the front
of the stage, near the lights, stood a slender young
man, in picturesque costume, and with very red
cheeks and coal-black, artificial curls. It was
Willie, my own never-to-be-forgotten Willie. Now
he ran both hands through his hair, rolled his
eyes like two fire-wheels, and cried: 'Wretches!
wretches! false, hypocritical crocodiles! Your
eyes are water — your hearts brass! Kisses on
your lips — swords in your bosoms!'

"Then the gray man put me to his lower lip,
and drew from me the shrillest sound, which went
to the bottom of my soul. And as if the whistle
which shrieked through the house had been a
preconcerted sign, there arose all at once such a
fiendish uproar as I never heard before. There
was whistling, hissing, stamping of feet, thump-
ing of canes, laughing, and screaming, till the

walls and ceiling shook. I saw my old friend stagger and beat his forehead with his doubled fist. Then the curtain fell. It was the last time that I ever saw my poor Willie. And I have never been able to learn what became of him. Good night."

"Good night, old fellow."

Man can accustom himself to anything, even to a talking key. On the following evening it seemed quite natural to expect a little gossip from the house-key before going to sleep, and my friend did not keep me waiting long.

"Do you know," he began, "that this afternoon, instead of remaining at your work, you spent two hours looking out the window?"

"Was it really two hours, house-key? Well, you see, I was tired of working; besides, the closeness of the room and the fresh air outside—"

"And the little seamstress in the attic room across the way," interrupted the house-key; "well, well, don't be angry. I am not going to preach you a sermon. You are old enough to know what to do and what not to do. But the sight of the neat, flaxen-haired person, plying her needle so industriously, brought to my mind an old story, which I would like to tell you."

"Let me hear it," I implored, and the house-
key began : —

"Years ago there lived in this house a seamstress, who was not unlike your opposite neighbor. She was a very young thing, and as pretty
as a picture; besides, she was as busy as a bee,
and merry as a crested lark in May. And she
sang like a lark while at her work, and lovely
songs, such as, for example, 'Enjoy life while
the light is still burning,' 'Three knights came
riding through the gate,' and 'Early in the morn
a little maid arose.' Altogether, it was rather
noisy in the house at that time, for, besides little
Lizzie, there were half a dozen other seamstresses,
fair-haired and dark, good and bad. They were
employed by a large woman with false curls and
a well-oiled tongue that went all day like a mill-
clapper.

"The poor things had to work busily, for their
employer kept a sharp watch over their fingers.
But she did not treat the young people altogether
badly, and what at first struck me as strange
was the strictness with which she watched over
the young girls' conduct. Indeed, evil tongues
were of the opinion that this happened more
from jealousy than from motherly anxiety, and
at last I almost came to think so too.

"At that time, just as now, there was a shoe-maker's shop on the ground floor; and I soon found out that the brown-haired foreman had his eye on little Lizzie. In spite of all madam's watchfulness, it occasionally happened that the two young people met on the steps. At such times the shoemaker usually said: 'Fine weather to-day, little miss'; and Lizzie would reply, 'Yes, very fine weather'; and then she would slip quickly past him like a shrew-mouse. My place was then on a nail out in the hall, and thus it happened that I could overlook the doorsteps. One morning — it was Lizzie's birthday — I saw the shoemaker creep up the stairs in the early dawn, before anybody was awake, and lay something gently on the floor before the young girl's door. People in love are wont to leave flowers at such a time. But the foreman's gift was not of that kind, but a pair of dainty, high-heeled shoes of polished leather, of which a princess might have been proud. Fortunately, the little maiden discovered them in safety before anybody else had seen them. How delighted she was! The shoes fitted perfectly, and the shoemaker had never taken her measure."

Here the house-key paused, and I concluded that he had reached a change in affairs.

"A short time after," the key went on to say,
"the stout woman who employed the seamstresses
received a visit from a young man of distinguished
bearing, who ordered a large quantity of fine
linen. The visit was repeated a day or two later,
and then oftener, and I soon knew that the young
count, for such he was, came to the house on
account of little Lizzie. Probably he had made
her acquaintance sometime when she was out
for a walk, for I noticed particularly that she
already knew him, I discovered too, to my dis-
appointment, that she was not indifferent to him;
and what disturbed me most was the fact that
the madam this time seemed to be blind.

"But the shoemaker on the ground floor was
not blind. Whenever the count entered the
house, the poor fellow would hammer away as
fiercely at his boot-sole as if he had his favored
rival under his hand.

"The last day of the year had come. On
New Year's eve the seamstresses were regularly
invited to take punch with their employer; and
so they were this time. In the course of the
afternoon the count had been there, and had
spoken in a low voice with little Lizzie in the
hall, and I had heard their conversation.

"The evening came, and soon the company were sitting around the big bowl of fragrant drink, and consuming great mountains of cake. I, too, was there, and was a person of no small importance. The maidens were going to pour lead, and one of them thought that the melted metal ought to be dropped through a church key, to make the charm effective. For want of a church key they had selected me, and I think, myself, without boasting, that I am about as good as a church key. What do you think?"

"You are the most dignified key I have ever met," I replied.

"Thank you," said the key, somewhat affected. "But let me go on.

"The lead was brought; it was lead from a church window. They melted it in an iron spoon, and then one after another poured the hot metal through my ring into a bowl filled with water. This caused much fun and laughter. Little Lizzie, too, who had sat the whole evening silent and absorbed, took the spoon and poured the lead. 'A shoemaker's chair!' cried one of the maidens, laughing. 'No, a count's crown!' said a second, making up a scornful face.

"Whereupon another play was begun, in which

I was also used. They fastened me to a thread
and suspended me in an empty glass. Then
some one would ask a question, and if I struck
against the glass once, they understood the
answer to be yes, and if more than once, no.

"Thus the time passed till midnight. The
bells were striking twelve from the tower; the
company wished one another a Happy New Year,
and then each of the young girls went to her
room. In the midst of breaking up no attention
was paid to me, and nobody saw that little
Lizzie seized me, and hid me in her pocket.

"When she reached her room she took a ball
of yarn from her work-basket and tied the end
of it, with trembling fingers, to my handle. Her
heart was beating loudly.

"'Wait,' she said softly to herself; 'I will first
ask Fate whether I ought to do it or not.' She
placed a glass on the table and suspended me
in it by the thread. 'Yes or no?' she asked
with quivering voice.

"If I had possessed the gift of human speech
then, I should surely have made use of it to
give her some good advice; but I had to see
in silence what danger the poor child was in.
'No,' thought I, 'she must be warned.' I made

myself as heavy as I possibly could, and — crack
— crack! — the thread had given way, and the
glass was broken to pieces.

"The maiden grew deathly pale, and shook
from head to foot. Trembling, she gathered up
the fragments; then she knelt down and prayed
a long, long time.

"After that she was calm. She put out the
light and went to bed. After a while footsteps
were heard in front of the house, and a low
whistle. Lizzie did not move, but buried her
little head in her pillow. But I saw, sitting at
the sleeping maiden's head the whole night long,
a little angel, who had two wings and carried
a lily in his hand."

"That sounds improbable, house-key."

"Improbable?" returned the house-key, grieved.
"Is it not far more improbable that a house-
key should tell you a story?"

Nothing could be said against that, and I
thought it advisable to keep silent.

"It only remains now for me to tell you," my
friend continued, "that the old woman who lets
this room to you is none other than the little
Lizzie of that time, and that her husband, the
old, white-haired shoemaker, is the same one

who placed a pair of high-heeled shoes in front
of the little seamstress' door.

"And to-morrow," the key went on to say,
" when we return from the *Green Hedgehog*
I will tell you how I came by the ability to
express myself in human speech. That is the
most wonderful story of all."

"To-morrow, dear house-key," I said, with
a sigh, "we shall hardly visit the *Green Hedgehog;* but I will listen with pleasure to your
gossip, over a cup of tea."

"Over a cup of tea?" asked the house-key,
drawling his words. "No, my friend, that would
not do. Know that I only talk when I have
spent the evening at the tavern."

"Then I must wait patiently till the first of
next month," I replied, disheartened.

The house-key muttered something I could not
understand, in his beard. A happy thought came
to me.

"Do you know what, old friend!" I said; "I
will, of course with your permission, put the
stories you have told me on paper, and send the
manuscript to a man who prints such things.
Perhaps, next month, we can have one or two
evenings more at the *Green Hedgehog.*"

" Do it," said the house-key.

THE FORGOTTEN BELL.

MANY, many years ago there was a pious hermit. He had turned his back on the world, and had built a hermitage in a green meadow, which lay in the midst of the forest; and the peasants of the neighboring villages and farms had helped him diligently in the building and furnishing of his hut. Next the hermit's dwelling stood a chapel with a doleful Madonna; and above it, under a little roof, hung a small bell, which the solitary man was accustomed to ring at certain hours, and this was his most important work of the day; the rest of the time he spent in prayer and pious reflection. His thirst he quenched at a cool fountain, which sprang up out of the black-wood earth, not far from the hermitage; but he satisfied his hunger with the fruit of the forest and the food which the faithful peasant women brought to him.

In this way the pious man lived for a long

succession of years. Then he laid himself down
on his bed of straw, wrapped himself up closely
in his cowl, and died. Many tears were shed at
his burial, and the sobbing women said, "Such
a hermit as he was we shall never have again."
And in this respect they were quite right.

It happened that soon after the hermit's de-
cease another came, who established himself in
the deserted hermitage; and he pleased the
women quite well, for he was young in years
and had a pair of eyes as black as coals.
But the new hermit was an eyesore to the
men; why, it was never exactly known. In
short, the peasants collected together one day,
seized the recluse, and conducted him to the
highway. And the hermit turned his back to
the thankless fellows, and was seen no more in
that region.

From that time the hermitage stood desolate,
and only occasionally did a roving huntsman, or
a maiden with her jug, turn their footsteps
towards the deserted house to draw refresh-
ment from the well near by. Brown wood-moss
grew luxuriantly on the thatched roof of the
hermitage, and brambles and clematis grew round
the door and windows. In the deceased hermit's

straw bed the field-mice were rearing their young, and in the chapel the red-tail had built her nest. The forest, with its creatures, was gradually taking possession again of the ground which man had taken away from it.

Spring was about to make her appearance, and the earth was getting ready for the Easter festival. With damp wings the thawing wind came flying across the sea, shook the trees and threw the fir-cones and dead branches on the ground. The springs and brooks murmured louder, and ran more swiftly on their winding way. The tips of the snowdrops and anemones peeped stealthily up out of the ground in the woods, and the showy laurel put on its red silk gown. Then came the hoopoo bird with his bright-colored crest and announced the coming of the cuckoo. And the briers shook off their last dry leaves and stood with their buds swollen with sap, waiting patiently for the awakening call of Spring.

The little bell in the ruined forest chapel saw with sorrow how everything was preparing for the feast of the Resurrection. In former years, when the sound of the bells trembled through the air at the happy Easter-tide, she, too, had lifted her voice and sung in the chorus of the proud sisters in the church towers. But that time was long ago. Since the old hermit was buried, no hand had pulled the rope at Easter-tide; silent and forgotten hung the bell beneath her little roof, and for a bell nothing is harder than to be obliged to keep silent at the feast of the Resurrection.

Passion week had come. On Wednesday the hare came bounding out of the forest. He stopped in front of the chapel, stood on his hind legs, and called up to the bell, " If you have anything to be done in the city, tell me, for I am on my way there. I have been appointed Easter hare, and have my paws full, and so much business to attend to that I don't know which end my head is on." The sorrowful bell kept silent, and the hare ran on.

The next night there was a mighty roaring in the air. The roes crouched down in the underbrush, for they thought it was the night huntsman passing through the forest. But it was not the forest fiend, but the bells, on their way to Rome to obtain the blessing of the Pope.

The bell from the convent on the mountain came over to the forest chapel, and stopped for a moment.

"How is it, sister," she asked the forgotten bell, "that you are not going, too?"

"Ah, I would gladly go," lamented the little bell. "But I have been idle the whole year long, therefore I dare not go with you. Still, if you will do me a favor, say a good word to the holy father in Rome for me. Perhaps he will send some one to ring me on Easter Sunday. It is so melancholy to have to be silent when all of you are singing. Will you do me the kindness?"

The convent bell mumbled something like "*non possumus.*" Then she arose, like a great, clumsy bird, from the ground, and flew after the others. And the forgotten bell remained sadly behind.

"Be thankful that human beings leave you in peace," said the forest owl to the bell. "The stupid beasts in the woods understand nothing about your ringing, and it disturbs me in my meditation. But you are not entirely forsaken, for I am going to build my nest near you. And you will gain much by it, for I am a man from whom you can learn a great deal." Thus spoke the owl, and puffed himself up. But the bell gave him no answer.

Easter morning dawned. Twilight still lingered over the village, and the mist stretched over

the mountain slope. A cool wind blew through
the branches of the trees, stirred the white May
lilies, and rustled through the dry reeds, so that it
sounded like the low tones of a harp. Then the
mountain tops grew red, and the firs creaked and
shook their branches, as if they were just awaking
from sleep. The sun rose and scattered gold over
the tips of the fir-trees, and the wood birds flapped
their wings, raised their voices, and sang their
Easter songs. But the forgotten bell hung sad
and silent under the roof in the chapel.

At the same hour a young man was walking
along the highway which led through the forest.
He wore a huntsman's leather jacket and a gray
hawk's feather in his hat. By his left side hung
a broad hunting-knife, with a handle of a stag's
horn; but instead of fire-arms, he carried a heavily
packed knapsack of badger's skin. This and a
cane of buckthorn with iron mountings, which he
swung in his right hand, led one to suppose that
the huntsman was not after game, but was making
a journey; and so it was.

At the place where a path which led to a mill
struck off from the road, the young fellow stopped,
and seemed undecided whether to keep on the
road or to take the meadow path. But he did not

linger long. He cast a gloomy look in the direction of the mill, threw his head back haughtily,
and gave a hunting-cry that made the fir-woods
resound. Then as he went along, he sang : —

> " Farewell, green jocund forest home !
> Thee must I leave behind me,
> Throughout the weary world to roam
> Till Fortune's favors find me.
> As hunter lad
> My joy I've had
> The noble stag in chasing;
> But now my way
> Leads to the fray
> Where death I shall be facing.

> " A gray hawk sat upon the height,
> Enchained by evil magic;
> In sadness pined he day and night,
> His mood was grim and tragic.
> He would exchange
> For freedom's range
> The forests' wide dominions;
> On high, on high,
> Thou wild bird, fly,
> And spread thy noble pinions."

But the last words stuck in the young man's
throat, and the half-suppressed sigh at the end ill
accorded with the huntsman's joyous manner.

Suddenly the youth left the broad road, and went diagonally through the forest, straight to the deserted hermitage. By the spring, which had its source near the house he stopped, bent down, and filled a wooden cup with the cool water. He drank it slowly, and sprinkled the last drops on the moss. "Well," he said, "now it is all over."

The water was clear and cold, but it could not cool the hot blood of the one who drank it. The young huntsman sat down on the threshold of the hermitage and covered his face with both hands.

The summer before, after a long absence, he had returned to the country, and entered the service of the old forester. He had seen something of the world; in the emperor's hunting-train, he had chased the chamois and the steinboc in the high mountains; he had followed his master to the merry hunting-boxes and to the splendid residence in the capital; and everywhere he had carried with him his love for the miller's fair-haired daughter in his native valley. He had come back with a generous sum of money and many sweet hopes, but they had melted away to nothing, and now he was on the point of leaving the country and enlisting as a soldier.

It was near the hermitage in the forest where he had found his sweetheart for the first time after their separation. She had come to draw water; and when the hunter recognized the beautiful, slender form, as she bent over the well, his joy was so great that he leaped from his hiding-place with a wild shout, and threw his arms around the frightened maiden. But she had pushed him roughly away from her, so that he fell backwards, and then she turned her back and went away.

Later on, the huntsman had tried once more to approach the miller's daughter. It was at the time of the harvest festival, when young and old march in bands to the dancing-ground. There the huntsman had waylaid the beautiful girl, and had come to meet her with a friendly greeting and a bouquet of clove pinks. But when she saw the youth coming towards her, she had turned around and gone back to the mill, and the hunter, in his anger, had thrown the bunch of pinks into the mill brook. The coy maid had fished the flowers out of the water near the dam, dried them, and laid them away in her chest, but he knew nothing about that.

Then perversity came over the huntsman. " If you go to the left, I will go to the right," he thought; and lest she might imagine that he took the matter to heart, he joined a company of gay fellows, drank, sang, and carried on so madly that the wild youth was in everybody's mouth for seven miles around.

That went on through the whole winter. Then one evening a bright light, which took the form of a sword, was seen in the sky, and shortly after the news came that in the spring there would be war in Italy. It was not long before the beating of drums was heard in the land, and the roads swarmed with travelling people, who were all going to join the imperial army. Then the hunts-man gave notice that he was going to leave the forester's service, gave his drinking-companions a generous parting cup, and followed the rest, to forget on the field his sorrow and distress. And he had already really come as far as the hermitage in the forest. He was now sitting on the door-stone, sadly hanging his head.

A soft, distant rustling in the underbrush fell on the young fellow's sharp ear. The huntsman was awake in him, and his sharp eye looked about for the cause of the sound. But it was no shift-ing game that was coming through the bushes. Between the trunks of the fir-trees gleamed some-

thing light, like a woman's garments, and the
hunter slipped noiselessly, but with loud-beating
heart, behind the wall of the house, for through
the forest came walking her whom he would fain
forget, but could not forget.

The maiden came slowly nearer. Now and
then she bent down to add a flower to the nosegay
which she carried in her hand, and each time her
long flaxen braids would fall forward and touch
the ground. When she reached the well, she filled
a little earthen jug with the water and placed the
nosegay in it. Then she went into the chapel,
placed the flowers before the image of the Virgin,
and knelt down on the moss-covered step.

In a low voice she repeated the angel's greeting, and then began to pour out her heart to
the queen of heaven. It was a prayer full of
self-accusation and repentance. " I have driven
him from me," she bemoaned, " driven him out
into danger and death, and yet I love him so!
more dearly than the light of my eyes! Still
there is time to change everything by a word of
reconciliation, if I knew that he still loved me.
Easter is the time of miracles. Give me, oh,
heaven, a sign, if he still thinks of me lovingly
and faithfully, and I will run after him to the

end of the world, and bring him back. Give
me a sign!"

Then above her softly sounded the bell. It
was only a single tone, but it rang through the
heart of the grieved maiden like a joyful song
of jubilee. She lifted her eyes and looked up
questioningly at the Madonna. Then the bell
sounded for the second time, and louder and
more joyful, and when the maiden turned, there
stood in the entrance of the chapel the young
huntsman, stretching out his arms to his beloved.
And this time she did not run away. She threw
her arms about the wild hunter's sun-burned
neck, and stammered words of love.

The titmice, and the golden-crested wrens
which lived in the branches of the fir-trees, fluttered along, and the wood-mouse put his head
out at the door of his house, and everything
looked curiously at the pair in the chapel.

The two remained in each others' embrace
for a long time. Then the huntsman grasped
the rope of the bell and called up to it: "Bell,
you have brought us together; now tell our joy
to the forest!" And the little bell under the
chapel roof began to gleam with joy in the
warm sunshine, and swung tirelessly to and fro
and let her clear voice sound through the forest.

From the towers in the surrounding villages
came the sounds of famous church bells. They
had returned the night before from their visit
to Rome, and had seen many wonderful sights.
But not one of them sang her Easter song so
joyfully as the little forgotten bell in the forest.

THE WATER OF YOUTH.

IT was Midsummer day and the heat of noon lay on the cornfields. Occasionally a fresh breeze blew down from the forest mountain; then the stalks would bend low, and the poppies on the border of the field would scatter their delicate petals. Crickets and grasshoppers made music in the grain, and from the hawthorn bushes on the boundary line came now and then the low call of the yellow-hammer.

Through the cornfield, which stretched from the valley to the mountain, along a narrow path a young peasant woman of slender, vigorous form, was walking. She wore the full gown customary in the country, and a red kerchief on her head to protect her from the sun's rays; a basket hung on her left arm, and in her right hand she carried a stone jug.

As soon as the gold-hammer in the hawthorn bush saw her, he flew to the topmost bough and greeted her with the cry, "Little girl, little girl, how are you!" But the bird was mistaken; the fair-haired Greta was no maiden, but a young wife, and she was now on her way to her husband, who was cutting wood over in the forest.

When the beautiful woman reached the edge of the woods she stopped to listen, and soon she heard the blows of an axe, towards which she was to turn her steps. It was not long before she caught sight of her husband, who was felling a fir-tree with mighty strokes, and she called to him in a joyful voice.

"Stand still, where you are!" he shouted back; "the tree is going to fall." And the fir-tree gave a deep groan, bent forward, and fell to the ground with a crash.

Then Greta came along, and the sun-burned wood-cutter took his young wife in his arms and kissed her fondly. Then they sat down on the trunk of a tree and took out the lunch that she had brought in the basket. Then Hans laid down his bread, seized his axe, saying, "I have forgotten something," and went to the stump of the tree he had just felled, and cut three crosses in the wood.

"Why do you do that, Hans?" asked his wife.

"That is for the sake of the little old women of the forest," the husband explained. "The poor little creatures have a wicked enemy, the wild huntsman. He lies in wait for them day and night, and hunts them with his dogs. But if the persecuted little women can escape to such a tree trunk, then the wild huntsman can do them no harm, on account of the three crosses."

The young wife opened her eyes wide. "Have you ever seen one of these little forest folk?" she asked, with curiosity.

"No; they seldom let themselves be seen. But this is Midsummer day, and then they are visible." And suddenly he called out in a clear voice into the forest, "Little forest woman, come forth!"

He had only done it to tease his wife. But on holy Midsummer day one should not make sport of such things in the forest.

Suddenly there stood before the young people a little woman about an ell high, of dainty form and beautiful face. She wore a long white dress, and a bunch of mistletoe in her yellow hair.

Hans and Greta were very much startled. They rose quickly from their seat, and Greta made a courtesy as well as she knew how.

"You called me at just the right time," said
the little creature, and pointed with her forefinger
at the sun, which stood exactly over her head;
"and one good turn" — here she pointed to the
stump with the three marks — "deserves another.
Gold and silver have I none to give you, but I
know something better. Come with me; no harm
will happen to you; and take your jug with you;
you will be able to use it."

Having spoken these words, she went on. Hans
shouldered his axe, Greta took up her stone jug,
and both followed the little woman. But she
walked exactly like a duck, and Greta pulled her
husband's arm, pointed to the little waddling
woman, and was going to whisper something in
his ear, but Hans laid his finger on his mouth.
Nothing hurts the little creatures more than to
have their gait made fun of. They have feet
like a goose, and that is why they wear long,
flowing skirts.

After a short time, the three came to an open
place in the woods. Primeval trees stood in a
circle around a meadow, in the grass grew lilies
and bluebells, and great butterflies sat on them,
opening and shutting their wings. And Hans,
who thought he knew the whole forest, could

not remember that he had ever been in this place before. On the border of the meadow stood a little house. The walls were covered with bark, and the roof was shingled with scales of fir cones, and each scale was fastened down with a rose-thorn. Here was the little woman's home.

She led her guests behind the house, and pointed to a well whose waters flowed noiselessly out of the black earth. Juicy colt's-foot and *fleur-de-lis* grew on its brink, and over the surface danced golden-green dragon-flies.

"That is the well of youth," said the little woman. "A bath in its waters makes an old man a boy and an old woman a young girl again. But if one drinks the water, it prevents him from growing old, and grants him the freshness of youth till death. Fill your jug and carry it home. But use the precious water sparingly: one drop every Sunday is sufficient to keep you young. And one thing more: if ever you, Hans, cast your eye on any other woman, or you, Greta, on any other man, the water will lose its power. Remember that. Now fill your jug, and farewell!"

The little creature spoke these words, pre-

vented the lucky pair from thanking her, and
went into her house. But Greta filled the jug
with the water of youth, and then hurried away,
as fast as she could go, to her own cottage.

When they reached home, Hans put the water
in a bottle, and sealed it with fir-resin. "For
the present," he said, "we have no use for the
water of youth, and we can save it; the time
will come soon enough when we shall need it."
And then they put the bottle in the cupboard,
where they kept their treasures, — a pair of old
coins, a string of garnet beads from which hung
a golden penny, and two silver spoons. "But,
Greta, now be sure and take care that the water
does not lose its strength!"

And what care they took! If the young forester passed by the garden, and exchanged a
greeting with Greta, as he was accustomed to
do, then Greta did not look up from her vegetable bed.   And when Hans sat in the *White
Stag* in the evening, and the pretty Lizzie brought
him the wine, he made up a face like a cat when
it thunders; and at last he gave up going to the
inn, and stayed at home with his wife. So the
water must surely keep its magic power.

Thus passed a year of love and happiness **to**

the young pair; for instead of two there were
three of them. In the cradle a little round boy
was kicking and screaming, till the father's
heart leaped for joy. "Now," he thought, "the
time has come for opening the bottle. What do
you think, Greta? A drop of the water of
youth will do you good."

His wife agreed with him, and Hans went to
the room where the magic drink was kept. With
his hands trembling for joy, he broke the seal,
and — oh dear! oh dear! the bottle slipped from
his grasp, and the drink of youth flowed over
the floor. A little more and Hans would have
fallen on the floor, too, for he was so frightened
at the misfortune. What should he do? On no
account should his wife know what had happened;
she might die from fright. Perhaps he would
tell her later what he had done; perhaps, too,
he might find the well of youth again, — which, to
be sure, he had sought for hitherto in vain, — and
repair the loss. He hastily filled a new bottle,
which was exactly like the first, with well-water;
and well-water it was too that he gave to his
wife.

"Ah, how that revives and strengthens me!"
said Greta. "Take a drop too, dear Hans."

And Hans obeyed, and praised the virtue of the
wonderful drink; and from that time on they
each took a drop when the bells were ringing
for church.   And Greta bloomed like a rose; as
for Hans, every vein in his body swelled with
health and strength.   But he put off the confes-
sion of his deed from day to day; for he secretly
hoped to find the well of youth again at last.
But roam through the woods as much as he
would, the meadow where the little old woman
lived he could not find.

Thus two years more passed by.   A little
girl had come to join the little boy, and Greta's
round chin had grown double.   She did not
notice it herself, for looking-glasses were not
known in those days.   Hans saw it, to be sure,
but he took care not to speak of it, and his love
for his portly wife redoubled.

Then came a misfortune; at least, Dame Greta
considered it so.   One day, when she was cleaning house, little Peter, her eldest, got into the
cupboard, where the bottle of the supposed water
of youth stood, clumsily upset it, so that it broke
and spilled the contents.

"Oh, merciful heavens!" bewailed the mother.
"It is lucky, though, that Hans is not at home!"

With trembling hands she gathered up the pieces
from the floor, and replaced the bottle with
another, which she filled with ordinary water.
— "The deception will surely be found out, for
now it is all over with the eternal youth. Oh
dear, oh dear!" — But she determined, above all,
not to let her husband notice anything unusual.

Again some time passed by, and the two
people lived together the same as on the day
that the priest joined their hands together. Each
carefully avoided letting the other notice that
youth was past, and every Sunday they con-
scientiously took the magic drop.

One morning, when the husband was combing his hair, it happened that he came across
a gray hair. And he thought, "Now the time
has come for me to tell my wife the truth." With
a heavy heart he began : "Greta, it seems to me
that our water of youth has lost its power. See!
I have found a gray hair. I am growing old."

Greta was startled; but she recovered herself,
and, with a forced laugh, cried : "A gray hair! I
was no more than ten years old when I had a
gray lock in my hair. Such a thing often happens. You have just been cleaning a badger;
perhaps you got some of the fat in your hair;

badger's fat is known to turn the hair gray.
No, dear Hans, the water still has its old power,
or," — here she gave him an anxious look — "or
do you think that I am growing old too?"

Then Hans laughed outright. "You — old?
You are as blooming as a peony!" And then
he threw his arms around her big waist and
gave her a kiss. But when he was by himself
he said with secret delight, "Thank the Lord!
She doesn't notice that we are growing old. So
I must have done right."

And his wife thought the same thing.

On the evening of the same day the young
people of the village danced to the fiddle of a
travelling musician, and no merrier couple turned
about the linden-tree than Hans and Greta. The
peasant women, to be sure, made sarcastic remarks about them, but the two happy people
heard none of their ridicule.

In the following autumn it happened, as Hans
was eating a Martinmas goose with his family,
Dame Greta broke out one of her teeth. Then
there was a great lament, for she had been
proud of her white teeth. And when the husband and wife were alone together, Greta said
in an unsteady voice, "Such a misfortune would
not have happened if the water — "

Then Hans began to scold. "You expect the water to help everything? Doesn't it often happen that a child, in cracking a nut, breaks out a tooth? What have you against the delicious water? Are you not as fresh and healthy as a young head of lettuce? Or have you cast your eyes on another, that you mistrust the water's virtue?"

Then his wife laughed, wiped the tears from her cheeks, and kissed her old man till he nearly lost his breath. In the afternoon they sat together on the stone seat in front of the house, and sang duets about true love, and the passersby said, "The silly old people!" but the happy pair did not hear them.

Thus passed many years. The house had become too small for the children; they had married and gone away, and had children of their own. The two old people were alone again, and were as much in love with each other as on the day of their wedding; and every Sunday, when the bells were ringing for church, they each took one drop out of the bottle.

Midsummer day was drawing near again. The evening before, Hans and Greta were sitting in front of the house, looking up towards

the hill where the Midsummer bonfire was
blazing; and from the distance sounded the
merry shouts of the young men and maidens, as
they poked the fire and jumped through the
flames in couples. Then the wife said, "Dear
Hans, I should like to go into the forest once
more. If you are willing, we will start early
to-morrow morning. But you must waken me,
for, at the time when the elderberries bloom,
young women are apt to sleep long after daylight."

Hans was agreed. The next morning he
woke his wife and they went together to the
woods. They walked along arm in arm, like
two lovers, and each carefully guarded the steps
of the other.

When Hans stepped cautiously over the root
of a tree, his wife would say, "Oh, Hans, you
jump like a young kid!" And when Greta
timidly crossed a little hole, her husband would
laugh, and cry, "Hold up your skirts, Greta!
hop!" Then they found an old fir-tree, and in
its shadow feasted on what Greta had brought
with her.

"Here it was," said Hans, "that the little old
woman once appeared to us, and over yonder must

lie the meadow with the well of youth. But I have
never been able to find meadow or well again."

"And, thank the Lord, that has not been necessary," hastily interrupted Greta, "for our bottle
is still far from empty."

"To be sure, to be sure," assented Hans. "But
I should be very much pleased if we could see
the good little woman once again and thank her
for our good fortune. Come, let us go and look.
Perhaps I may be as lucky to-day as before."

Then they rose and went into the deep forest,
and behold! after a quarter of an hour, before
their eyes shone the sunny forest meadow! Lilies
and harebells bloomed in the grass, bright butterflies flew hither and thither, and on the edge of
the woods still stood the little house just as
years before. With beating hearts they went
round the house, and sure enough, there was the
well of youth too, with the golden-green dragon-
flies hovering over it.

Hans and Greta stepped up to the brink of
the well. Taking each other by the hand, they
bent over the water — and out of the clear mirror of the spring, two gray heads, with kindly,
wrinkled faces, looked back at them.

Then hot tears rushed to their eyes, and stammering and sobbing they confessed their guilt, and it was some time before it became clear to them that each had deceived the other, and for long years had cheated one another for love's sake.

"Then you knew that we were both growing old?" cried Hans, with delight.

"To be sure, to be sure," said his wife, laughing in the midst of her tears.

"And so did I," exulted the old Hans; and he tried to leap for joy. Then he took Greta's head in his hands and kissed her just as he had done when she promised to be his wife.

And, as if she had grown up out of the ground, the little forest woman stood before the two old people.

"Be welcome!" she said. "You have not been to see me for a long time. But, but," continued the little woman, shaking her finger at them, "you have not taken good care of the water of youth. Wrinkles and gray hairs, indeed! Now," she continued, consolingly, "those are easily remedied, and you have come at a propitious hour. Quick! Jump into the well — it is not deep — and plunge your gray heads under, then you will see a miracle. The bath will give you the strength of youth and beauty again. But be quick, before the sun goes down!"

Hans and Greta looked at each other inquiringly. "Will you?" asked the husband in an unsteady voice.

"Never!" quickly answered Greta. "Oh, if you only knew how happy I am, that at last I may dare to be old. And then it would not do, on account of our children and grandchildren. No, dear little woman; a thousand thanks for your kindness, but we will remain as we are. Is it not so, Hans?"

"Yes," replied Hans; "we will remain old. Hurrah! If you knew, Greta, how becoming your gray hair is!"

"As you like," said the little creature, a bit hurt. "Nothing is compulsory here." Thus she spoke, and went into her house and closed the door behind her.

But the two old people kissed each other again. Then they went arm in arm on their homeward way through the forest, and the midsummer sun poured a golden gleam about their gray heads.

THE FOUR EVANGELISTS.

HIS name was Gustavus Adolphus, and he was
the son of the clock-maker Lacknail, who
led a modest life in a little town. Gustavus
Adolphus wished to become a clergyman, and had
begun very early to devote his services to the
church: he rang the bells on Sunday; at first the
little ones, and then afterwards, when he became
strong enough, the large ones; and when the
congregation found edification in singing, he blew
the organ with holy zeal, till the perspiration rolled
down over his forehead. Then, too, he buried the
dead bodies of pet birds and rabbits under the
cabbage-heads in his parents' vegetable garden,
and preached such touching discourses over them
that tears came into the eyes of the listening
washerwomen, who were working by the brook
which flowed past.

At school, he was frankly none of the best. He
was thick-headed, and learned but slowly how to

read, write, and reckon; but the catechism he had
at his tongue's end, and he knew a little trick, too;
that is, he could repeat "Our Father," as rapidly
backwards as forwards, and none of his schoolmates could emulate him in that. Besides, Gustavus Adolphus was no devotee, nor hypocrite, but
he was a good-natured, honest fellow, whom everybody could endure.

Whenever the boy spoke in the presence of his
parents of wishing to become a clergyman, his
father would knit his brows, not because he was
opposed to the calling as such, but because in consid-
eration of his modest income he feared the expense
of such an education. But his mother smiled with
delight at the thought of seeing her son one day
in the pulpit, and when the principal of the town
school once told her plainly that Gustavus Adolphus was of too limited capacity to be able to
study, she went away indignant, and would not
believe it.

But the matter had one difficulty. Gustavus
Adolphus had what is called a stammering tongue,
and could not pronounce certain letters well; for
example, R and S gave him great trouble. One
day he read in his reading-book of the celebrated
orator Demosthenes, who had to contend with a

similar impediment, and he at once determined to imitate him. Like him, he no longer cut his hair, but went every day to the roaring mill-dam and declaimed in a loud voice, "John the silly soap-suds stirrer."

Indeed, his indefatigable perseverance would have surely made him a pulpit orator, if Providence had not frustrated his plans. His mother, who till now had taken his part, laid her down and died. His father spoke the word of command, and Gustavus Adolphus entered his father's workshop as a clock-maker's apprentice. There the poor young fellow had to sit, with shaded eyes, and was obliged to clean and oil the clocks of his fellow-townsmen; and, in his opinion, there was no more unfortunate creature to be found on God's earth than Gustavus Adolphus Lacknail.

Time heals all things. He learned to become resigned; and when the winding of the clock in the church tower was intrusted to him, he was half reconciled to his fate.

The years passed away one after another Gustavus Adolphus had served his time and went out as a journeyman. But he did not go beyond the next town, and returned home as soon as the required term had expired. For a year or two he worked on as his father's assistant; then his father departed this life, and he was master in the business, and the business prospered.

Soon after, the place of sexton in the town church was vacated. To the astonishment of all the inhabitants Gustavus Adolphus sought the position, and obtained it, too. Evil tongues said that a contemptible love of gain lead the wealthy man to this step; but when it became known that the new church sexton had made over his salary to the poor-house, then the slanderers were silent, and Gustavus Adolphus' reputation grew like the crescent moon. The pastor brought it about that Mr. Lacknail received the title of "assistant." This sounded better than "sexton."

Henceforth Gustavus Adolphus was never seen in public except in a long black coat, which he wore buttoned up to the neck; above the collar, however, appeared a modest white cravat, and above this a round, smoothly shaven face, about whose mouth constantly played a kindly smile.

Gustavus Adolphus was reconciled to his fate. The dreams of his boyhood years were not fulfilled, to be sure; he was not the first person in the church, but unquestionably the second; for the organist, to whom this rank properly belonged, took his drams secretly, and on this account did not stand well in the community.

That the new assistant, soon after entering his office, should wed a Christian maiden seemed sensible to the people; but when, after a year and a day, he stood beaming with joy by the baptismal font, over which was held a little screaming Lacknail, then they all shook their heads, and the pastor as well, for the happy father, disregarding all the customary baptismal names, had chosen the name of Matthew for his first-born. Gustavus paid no heed to the people's talk, and took great delight in the little Matthew's growth.

Again joy entered the house of Mr. Lacknail; a second son was born to him; and when the pastor asked by what name the child should be baptized, the father said, proudly smiling, "Mark." Then it was evident what Mr. Lacknail was striving after; and he did not deny it; he had no other intention than to surround himself with the four evangelists.

Really, Heaven seemed to favor the honest man's intention, for after a year and a half a struggling Luke joined Matthew and Mark; and, moreover, a year later Mr. Lacknail dared to hope that he should shortly reach the goal of his desires.

But who would have thought the expected child capable of such wickedness! It came, came in good time; but it came into the world a maiden.

Then was Gustavus Adolphus very much grieved. At first he was angry with Providence, and would not even look at the child, — it bore the name of Elizabeth, — but then he scolded himself severely for his ingratitude, behaved henceforth towards the little one as it became a father and a servant of the church, and placed his hopes on the next child. But this was still worse than the last — that is, it stayed away entirely. One year passed after another; Matthew, Mark, and Luke grew to sturdy lads, and the coming of the fourth evangelist, John, was still looked forward to.

Then a consuming malady came to the little town, and among others Mrs. Lacknail fell a victim to it. When the year of mourning was over, the widower thought seriously of marrying again, that he might possibly yet possess a John; but the children dissuaded him from his intention, and Gustavus Adolphus remained a widower.

The young Lacknails prospered. Matthew was already studying, and what else but theology; Mark went to the seminary; Luke worked in his father's workshop; and Elizabeth kept the house. She was a beautiful, slender maiden, with a fresh, round face, and thick, blonde braids; and when Lacknail, now advancing in life, looked at her, he smiled, and laughed to himself. He had a design for his daughter, but he did not say what it was.

At that time the handsomest young man in the town and country round was head-waiter in the inn of the *Wild Man.* His name was "Jean," but they pronounced it "Zhang." To the affability which graces the brotherhood of waiters he united the polite manners of a diplomatist; he wore his blonde beard like the captain of a ship, and his curly hair was parted evenly from his forehead to the nape of his neck. Besides, he always wore snow-white linen, very conspicuous cuffs, and shirt-studs of aluminium as large as a dollar. Indeed, he was a splendid young man. Then, too, it was rumored about in the town that he rejoiced in a pretty little property, and that he intended sometime to purchase the *Wild Man.* So it really was not to be wondered at that the hearts of the townspeople's daughters beat more loudly when the handsome Jean greeted them as he passed by.

Just as skilful as the young man was in going

about with plates and glasses, just so unskilful
he had been for some time in handling his watch.
Hardly a week passed that his chronometer did
not need the help of Mr. Lacknail; sometimes
the crystal was cracked, sometimes the spring
was broken. Then Jean always took care to
give the patient with his own hands to the physician, and when discharged well, to take it
promptly away again; and in coming and going
it seldom failed to happen that the kitchen door
opened a little, and in the crack appeared a
pretty maiden's head, which nodded sweetly, and
then disappeared.

On fine Sundays, when the afternoon service
was over, Mr. Lacknail was wont to take a walk
with his daughter to the so-called huntsman's
house, where the people of the town amused
themselves by playing ninepins. Mr. Lacknail
never played, for he did not think it consistent
with his position; but he was not averse to a
good drink of beer, especially if it was seasoned
with sensible conversation, and this seasoning
for some weeks had been supplied by Jean, the
head-waiter. What a cultivated young man he
was, and what a knowledge he had of the world!
And moreover, he was a proper, steady man, and

went regularly to church on Sundays, and carried a gilt-edged singing-book in his hand.

The fair-haired Elizabeth grew happier each day, and sang at her work like a sky-lark. But her father became more and more silent and thoughtful.

And it happened one Sunday about noon, that the handsome Jean turned his steps towards Mr. Lack::ail's house. He was dressed in black and had a red pink in his buttonhole, which looked from a distance like a badge. On his curly head he wore a hat that shone like a mirror, on his hands straw-colored gloves, and over his left arm hung a dove-colored overcoat lined with brown silk. And the people who saw him passing, put their heads together and said: "Now he is going to propose to Elizabeth. What a lucky girl she is!"

The people were not mistaken. Jean found the father, who had already laid aside his official robe, and was smoking his pipe in a comfortable dressing-gown, alone in the sitting-room. The young man expressed his desire in appropriate language. He spoke of his love for Elizabeth, and then dexterously turned the conversation to the state of his finances. He had already taken a little package of papers from his breast pocket, when Mr. Lacknail said in a serious, almost melancholy voice: "Sit down, young man; I have something to tell you." And Jean sat down in confusion on the edge of a chair.

Mr. Lacknail began talking. He expatiated on the dreams of his youth, and his disappointed hopes, — things which are sufficiently well known to us. Then he went on to say: —

"You know, dear Mr. Zhang, that it was my dearest wish to call a fourth son mine; I should have had him baptized John. Heaven was not willing; it gave me a daughter instead of the longed-for son. She is a dear, good child, the joy of my old age, and to see her happy is my daily prayer. But I made an oath, an oath which now, since I have made your acquaintance, dear Zhang, I almost regret, for it separates you and my Elizabeth forever. I have sworn this, that my daughter shall only marry a man who is named John, and therefore she can never become the wife of a Zhang." Having spoken thus, Mr. Lacknail hung his head sorrowfully.

But Jean jumped up from his seat like a shuttlecock. "And is the name the only hindrance?" he asked.

"The only one; I swear it to you."

Jean stood as though he were transfigured. Then he took a paper out of his breast pocket, unfolded it, and laid it before the old man. "Read, Mr. Lacknail," he said, triumphantly.

The latter took the paper in surprise and read, "Sponsor for John Obermüller — "

He read no further. The paper fell from his hands, and his voice failed him. "And this John Obermüller?" he asked, finally, in a trembling voice.

"I am he!" said the happy waiter, exultingly. "Jean and John are exactly the same."

"O thou benignant Heaven!" cried Mr. Lacknail, folding his hands. "You have at last sent me a John. But, dear John, what unchristian tongue has so distorted the beautiful name of the evangelist?"

"That is French," explained the suitor; "but I promise you solemnly that in future I will always be called John instead, if I attain the object of my desires."

"Give me your hand on it, John," said Mr. Lacknail. Then he opened the door and called, "Elizabeth, come in here!" And a few moments later the two were in each other's embrace, and the third was wiping his eyes.

The happiness of the betrothed, the joy of the father when he went to church with his four evangelists to attend the wedding, and what followed — all that the reader must picture to himself; my pen is not equal to it.

At the present time Mr. John Obermüller is the proprietor of the inn of the *Wild Man,* and the plump wife Elizabeth stands faithfully by his side. They already have two big boys; the larger one is called Peter, the little one James, and it is said in the town that the couple have resolved to present the grandfather by degrees with the twelve apostles.

THE DISAPPOINTED DWARF.

WHERE the mountains, even in summer, wear caps of snow, where the hare in winter puts on a white coat, and the crows have yellow bills, there grows a beautiful tree called the Siberian pine, and out of its wood the people on the mountains carve animals, both wild and domestic, and sell them to the city people for hard cash.

Such a tree, and assuredly a primeval one, stood, and probably still stands to-day, on a lonely slope, where, in summer, thousands and thousands of Alpine roses bloom. From its branches hung long, gray beards of moss, and its mighty roots grasped weather-beaten boulders, between which the narrow entrance to a cave could be seen. The cave was inhabited, too, but it was neither a badger nor a bear that dwelt there, but a gnome, a timid dwarf.

He had seen better days. In the good old

times, which even mountain spirits look back to
with regret, he wore a golden crown, and the
name of Laurin, the king of the dwarfs, was
known in Germany and in Italy. The whole
range of mountains, with their underground
marvels, was his, and in the upper world he
had laid out a pleasure garden for his enjoyment,
where the most glorious roses shed their perfume,
and from the roses hung little golden bells, which
rang sweetly in the wind. But his underground
treasures and his beautiful garden did not sat-
isfy the dwarf. He yearned for a woman's love,
and, violent as he was, he stole away the beautiful Similde von Steier, to make her queen of
the dwarfs; and that was his ruin.

Mourning and weeping sat the stolen beauty in
the magic castle of the mountain, and all the
jewels which the dwarf laid at her feet could not
turn her thoughts. But it grew still worse. One
day when King Laurin visited his pleasure garden,
there arose from the crushed roses the huge forms
of giants in armor, and Dietleib, poor Similde's
betrothed, and his master, the mighty Dietrich
of Berne, fell upon him with their swords till he
lost sight and hearing. They set free the stolen
Similde and took the dwarf away with them

prisoner, and compelled him to serve as jester at
the court of Lombardy for the amusement of his
captors. All this happened many hundred years
ago, and stands written in detail in an ancient
book. Later, when everything was topsy-turvy in
Italy, Laurin was released, and ever after he dwelt
in the wilderness, a solitary, embittered, mountain
dwarf.

Usually, whenever he slipped out of his cavern,
and sat sunning himself under the Siberian pine-
tree, he wore his magic cap which made him
invisible, but sometimes he took it off, and thus
it happened that the people on the mountain knew
him very well. Shepherds, root-diggers, huntsmen,
and other honest people had often seen him, as he
sat on the mountain-side, and gazed listlessly into
the blue distance. He appeared there like a little
man about an ell high, with wrinkled face and
long, gray beard, and because he generally stayed
under the pine-tree, the people, who knew nothing
of his splendid past, called him "Zirbel."

People tell of kindly gnomes who make presents
to poor people of fir cones or the branches of
trees, which afterwards change to gold. The
sullen Zirbel did nothing of that sort, but, on the
other hand, he never played tricks on anybody,

but let the people who passed to and fro in his wilderness go their way unmolested. And thus many years passed by.

One day Zirbel was lying, as he often did, under his tree, sunning himself in the morning sunlight, and gazing up at the circle of white, snow-covered mountains, and the gold cloud-boats gliding along slowly in the sky.

Two mortals came climbing up the mountain, and the dwarf quickly put on his magic cap. It was an old peasant with a young, rosy-cheeked maiden, — father and daughter. Both were heavily laden, but they walked easily up the mountain under their burdens.

Above the old pine-tree, where there is a hollow place in the mountain, the old man stopped and said, " Lisi, we will stay here "; and then he began to fashion a house. He piled up stones, and out of branches and large pieces of bark, which he broke off from the fallen, decaying trunks, he built a hut, large enough to shelter a man from wind and rain. In the mean while the maiden was not idle, but filled a basket with flowers; these she thought of selling in the *Blue Steinboc* down below.

The *Blue Steinboc* — this was the name of an

Alpine inn, which stood about three miles distant
from the pine-tree — was full of summer visitors,
who were enjoying the mountain air and water,
caught trout, and feasted on venison which was
really only mutton. They wore jaunty feathers in
their hats, and gave many bright silver pieces for
edelweiss and little twigs of the sweet-scented rue.
The flowers they put in their red pocket-books,
and afterwards, at home, told of the dangers they
experienced in gathering them.

The dwarf regarded the beautiful maiden with
satisfaction, and for the first time in many years
a friendly grin passed over his face.

When the sun reached the zenith the old man
had finished his work. He called the maiden,
and they two ate the dinner she had brought with
her. Then the beautiful girl departed and went
with her basket down into the valley, while her
father stayed behind and went about his work. He
was a pitch-burner by trade, and had built his
hut on the mountain in order to gather the pitch
oozing from the evergreen trees.

The next day the fair-haired Lisi came back
again to bring food to her father and to gather
flowers. But Zirbel had stirred the earth-fires
during the night; thousands and thousands of

flowers had sprung up, and now stars and bells fresh with dew adorned the green pasture in such abundance that the maiden was able to reap a rich harvest. The dwarf followed closely on her footsteps, unseen, and took delight in her diligence, often coming so near her that he might have brushed her flaxen hair with his hand; but this he did not do lest he should frighten the charming child. When Lisi went away again, he stood on a rock a long time, looking after her; then he crept contented into his crevice and waited with delight for the next morning.

The morning came and the lovely Lisi came too; but with her came another, a dark lad in hunting-dress; and when Zirbel saw him, he made up a face as though he had bitten a green crab-apple.

The young huntsman had his arm around the lovely girl's waist, and in this way they came up to the old man, who was sitting before his hut, and the old man seemed to approve of their familiarity, for when they kissed each other he laughed; but everything turned green and yellow before the dwarf's eyes. Then the young people sat down on the trunk of a tree and sang songs of true love, and the father hummed softly with them, and then they began to bill and coo again like two pigeons.

These were terrible hours for poor Zirbel, and he would have liked to come between the pair with thunder and lightning, but he restrained himself. At last the lovers took their departure and went away together, while the father stood on the mountain-side and gazed after them.

Then suddenly there stood before him, as though sprung up out of the ground, Zirbel, the dwarf. The old man was indeed frightened, but he collected himself, and took off his hat with a bow and a scrape.

"Do you know me?" asked the dwarf.

"You are none other than Herr Zirbel," replied the pitch-burner. "Pardon me if I do not call you by your right name."

"Zirbel; yes; that is what they call me. And what is your name?"

"Peter."

"Well, Master Peter, you have a beautiful daughter — "

"Have you seen her?" interrupted the father with delight. "Beautiful she is, and good she is, too; but," he continued with a sigh, "poor, — poorer than a church mouse; and her lover, the

huntsman, has nothing but his strong limbs. —
O Herr Zirbel! Don't you know some buried
treasure or a gold mine or something else? That
would be very convenient for the dowry."

The dwarf nodded his head emphatically.
"Come with me, Master Peter, if you are not
afraid; I will show you something that will
make your mouth water."

Peter did not have to be asked a second time.
He threw his bag over his shoulder, and with
joyful expectation followed Zirbel, who went on
ahead.

At the foot of the old tree the dwarf stopped.
"The way is in through there," he said, pointing to the entrance of the cavern. "Come after
me, Master Peter!" Having said this he slipped
like a marmot into the den, and the pitch-burner
crept in behind him. At first the entrance was
very narrow, and Peter gave his head a hard bump
twice; but soon the hole grew wider, and after
a short time they reached a high, roomy cave,
and it was light here, too, for blue flames flickered on every side.

"Now just look about you!" commanded the
dwarf; and the old man did as he was told, but
it was some time before his eyes became accus-

tomed to the glittering splendor. A network of
threads of gold covered the walls, and from the
ceiling hung points of silver, wonderfully formed,
like stalactites. On the floor of the cave stood
a large copper kettle, filled to the brim with
heavy pieces of silver. Oh, how Peter opened
his eyes at this!

But the dwarf began to speak, saying, " All
the treasures that you see hoarded here shall be
your daughter's wedding portion — on one con
dition."

"Let me hear it, Herr Zirbel!" cried the
father, wild with delight.

"Your daughter," said the dwarf impressively,
"must give up the huntsman and — "

"Herr Zirbel, that cannot be."

"It must be. I will give the huntsman as
much silver as he can carry to compensate him,
— such a young fellow will easily console himself with another pretty girl, — and I will provide
another husband for your daughter. To be
plain, Master Peter, I myself will be your son-
in-law. Have you any objection to that?"

The pitch-burner was greatly frightened, but
he composed himself; with rich men and gnomes
it is not well to quarrel. "Herr Zirbel," he

said, "I, for my part, have nothing against you;
you are a man in the prime of life, and are able
to take care of a wife; but — maidens see with
different eyes from old graybeards. Do you
understand me?"

But Zirbel went on talking to the old man,
and at the same time scooped up silver pieces
out of the kettle, letting them fall back again
like rain, till poor Peter's head was all in a
whirl. Suddenly a bright thought came to him.
He appeared as if he were going to give his con-
sent, and said artfully: —

"Well, Herr Zirbel, I will take you to my
daughter. You shall see her at home, at her
work; and then, if you still wish to make her
your wife, I will, as her father, say 'yes and
amen,' and bring the maiden to you whenever
you please. For the huntsman you must give
me as much silver as I can carry away on my
back. But if you, of your own free will, back
out of the undertaking, then the money shall
be mine. Here is my bag — if you are agreed,
allow me to fill it immediately with your silver."

Zirbel was highly delighted with this proposition. He shoved the silver pieces into the bag
with his own hands, and on the top he laid a

sparkling bracelet as a bridal gift. Then they crept out into the daylight again, and Peter shouldered the precious burden. The dwarf took his future father-in-law by the arm and walked along beside him.

After they had been gone a good half hour, they came into the vicinity of the summer resort, the *Blue Steinboc.* They passed guide-posts and rustic seats bearing such names as Elsa's Rest, Olga's Seat, Adele's Hill, and other inscriptions, and suddenly they saw the bright garments of a woman gleaming through the trees.

"I will make myself invisible," said Zirbel, putting on his magic cap. Then both stepped nearer.

The woman's back was turned towards the wanderers. She was sitting on a camp-stool, and had a frame before her, such as Zirbel had never seen before. With curiosity he approached the lady with his companion, and looked at what she was doing. On a frame stood a tablet, which she had painted over, green on the lower part, and blue on the upper part; in the background was something like a white nightcap; in the foreground a rose-colored beast with horns and a bell at the neck.

"What is she doing?" asked Zirbel.

"She is painting," replied Peter. "She paints the mountains, the trees, animals, and people. Just look at it closely, Herr Zirbel. That white thing is the mountain yonder with its snow, and the red beast is a cow."

Zirbel examined the painting, and shook his big head thoughtfully; then he said:—

> "Master Peter, tell me, pray,
> Does Lisi too paint pictures gay?"

And Peter replied:—

> "Pictures all the day paints she,
> Greener far than celery."

Then the dwarf muttered something in his beard that Peter did not understand, and drew his companion away with him.

It was not long before they met a second lady; she was sitting on a moss-covered rock, and gazing with glassy eyes up at the blue sky. In her left hand she had a book, on which was written in golden letters, "Poetry," and in her right hand she held a pencil, with which she occasionally wrote something in the book. After a while she arose and read in a loud voice:—

> " Ah, if I were a birdling free,
>   Ah, if I soared on tiny wing,
>   Beloved, in my bill I'd bring
>   A sweet forget-me-not to thee.''

" What is the poor thing trying to do?" asked the dwarf compassionately.

" She is making poetry," explained Peter. "She is a poetess; that is, she makes rhymes, writes them in her book, and reads them aloud."

Then Zirbel whispered anxiously : —

> " Master Peter, truly tell,
>   Does lovely Lisi rhyme as well?"

And Peter replied : —

> " When she is tired of painting, 'tis true
>   She scribbles rhymes and reads them too."

"Oh dear!" said Zirbel, with a deep sigh. "Come, let us go along." And they went on.

The sun went down to the edge of the mountains, the birds stopped singing, and through the forest sounded the bells of the home-returning cattle. Through the fir-trees appeared the shingled roof of the *Blue Steinboc*, and from all sides the hungry guests were hurrying towards the hospitable abode. All of a sudden, as Peter and

his invisible companion came within a few steps
of the house, there sounded through the evening
stillness such a clangorous jangling and drum-
ming that Zirbel started in affright.

"Don't be afraid," said the old man, assuringly.
"If you get up on the stone seat and look in at
the window, you will see where the noise comes
from."

The dwarf got up on the bench, and looked
into the lighted hall. "I see two women," he
said softly, "who are pounding around with
their hands on a chest. Oh, it is horrible to see,
and still more horrible to hear! Tell me, Peter,
what it means."

"What does it mean?" replied the pitch-
burner. "They are playing the piano-forte, as
it is called."

Then said Zirbel, in a trembling voice:—

> "Master Peter, tell me in short,
> Does Lisi play the piano-forte?"

And Peter answered:—

> "If she can't paint or rhyme, she'll play
> On her piano the livelong day."

The dwarf groaned like a falling tree, and became silent.

"Herr Zirbel," suggested Peter after a while, in a suppressed voice, "Herr Zirbel, we ought to be going."

No answer.

The old man felt about in the place where the voice of the invisible dwarf had last come from, but his hand only grasped the air.

He called louder, "Herr Zirbel, where are you? It will soon be night, and we have still far to go."

Then there came a gust of wind from the mountain, and these words fell on Peter's ear: —

> "Master Peter, the bag is thine,
> But you may keep your daughter fine."

The crafty Peter would have leaped for joy, if the heavy bag of silver had not prevented him. He waved his hat gratefully in the direction from which the words had sounded, then he started along, and hurried as fast as he could towards the valley.

The story is ended, for you can easily imagine what happened further. The beautiful Lisi kept her huntsman, and if they are not dead —

But the dwarf Zirbel was unmarried, and remained so to his dying day.

THE EGYPTIAN FIRE–EATER.

"NEXT Easter he must go to N —— to school.
— Fact. — It is high time; he is eleven
years old, and here he is running wild with the
street-boys. — That's what I say."

He, that is, I, hung my head, and I felt more
like crying than laughing. I had passed eleven
sunny boyhood years in the little country town, I
stood in high esteem among my playmates, and
would rather be the first in the ranks of my birth-
place than second in the metropolis.

Through the gray mist, which surrounded my
near future like a thick fog, gleamed only one
light, but a bright, attractive light; that was the
theatre, the splendor of which I had already
learned to know. The white priests in the "Magic
Flute," Sarastro's lions, the fire-spitting serpents,
and the gay, merry Papageno, — such things could
not be seen at home; and when my parents promised me occasional visits to the theatre, as a re-

ward for diligence in study and exemplary conduct,
I left the Eden of my childhood, half consoled.

Young trees, transplanted at the proper time,
soon take root.   After a tearful farewell to my
friends and a slight attack of home-sickness, I was
quite content.   I was received into the second
class at the gymnasium, and drank eagerly of the
fountain of knowledge; a certain Frau Eberlein,
with whom I found board and lodging, cared for
my bodily welfare.

She was a widow, and kept a little store, in
which, with the assistance of a shop-girl, she served
customers, who called from morning to night.   She
dealt principally in groceries and vegetables, but
besides these, every conceivable thing was found
piled up in her shop: knitting-yarn, sheets of pictures, slate-pencils, cheese, pen-knives, balls of twine,
herring, soap, buttons, writing-paper, glue, hair-
pins, cigar-holders, oranges, fly-poison, brushes,
varnish, gingerbread, tin soldiers, corks, tallow
candles, tobacco-pouches, thimbles, gum-balls, and
torpedoes.   Besides, she prepared by means of
essences, peach brandy, maraschino, ros solis, and
other liqueurs, as well as an excellent ink, in the
manufacture of which I used to help her.   She
rejoiced in considerable prosperity, lived well, and
did not let me want for anything.

My passion for the theatre was a source of great
anxiety to good Frau Eberlein. She did not have
a very good opinion of the art in general, but
the comedy she despised from the bottom of her
heart. Therefore she made my visiting the theatre
as difficult as possible, and it was only after long
discussions, and after the shop-girl had added her
voice, that she would hand over the necessary
amount for purchasing a ticket. The shop-girl was
an oldish person, as thin as a giraffe which had
fasted for a long time, and was very well read.
She subscribed regularly to a popular periodical
with the motto, "Culture is freedom," and Frau
Eberlein was influenced somewhat by her judg-
ment. This kind-hearted woman was friendly
towards me, and as often as her employer asked,
"Is the play a proper one for young people?"
she would answer, "Yes," and Frau Eberlein would
have to let me go.

Those were glorious evenings. Long before it
was time for the play to begin, I was in my seat
in the gallery, looking down from my dizzy height,
into the house, still unlighted. Now a servant
comes and lights the lamps in the orchestra. The
parquet and the upper seats fill, but the reserved
seats and the boxes are still empty. Now it sud-

denly grows light; the chandelier comes down
from an opening in the ceiling. The musicians
appear and tune their instruments. It makes a
horrible discord, but still it is beautiful. The
doors slam; handsomely dressed ladies, in white
cloaks, gay officers, and civilians in stiff black
and white evening dress take their seats in the
boxes. The conductor mounts his elevated seat
and now it begins. The overture is terribly long,
but it comes to an end. Ting-aling-aling, — the
curtain rises. Ah! —

I soon decided in my own mind that it should
be my destiny, sometime, to delight the audience
from the stage, but I was still undecided whether
I would devote myself to the drama or the opera,
for it seemed to me an equally desirable lot to
shoot charmed bullets in "Der Freischütz" or,
hidden behind elderberry bushes, to shoot at
tyrannical Geslers in "William Tell." In the
mean time I learned Tell's monologue, "Along
this narrow path the man must come," by heart,
and practised the aria, "Through the forest,
through the meadows."

Providence seemed to favor my plan, for it
led me into an acquaintance with a certain Lipp,
who, on account of his connections, was in a
position to pave my way to the stage.

Lipp was a tall, slender youth, about sixteen years old, with terribly large feet and hands. He usually wore a very faded, light-blue coat, the sleeves of which hardly came below his elbows, and a red vest. He had a rather stooping gait, and a beaming smile continually played about his mouth. Besides, the poor fellow was always hungry, and it was this peculiarity which brought about our acquaintance.

On afternoons when there was no school, and I went out on the green to play ball with my companions or fly my kite, Frau Eberlein used to put something to eat in my pocket. Lipp soon spied it out, and he knew how to get a part, or even the whole of my luncheon for himself. He would pick up a pebble off the ground, slip it from one hand to the other several times, then place one fist above the other, saying : —

> " This hand, or that?
> Burned is the tail of the cat.
> Which do you choose?
> Upper or under will lose ! ''

If I said " upper," the stone was always in the lower hand, and *vice versa*. And Lipp would take my apple from me with a smile, and devour it as if he were half famished.

Why did I allow it? In the first place, because
Lipp was beyond me in years and in strength, and
in the second place, because he was the son of a
very important personage. His father was nothing
less than the door-keeper of the theatre; a splendid
man with a shining red nose and coal-black beard
reaching to his waist. The wise reader now knows
how young Lipp came by a light blue coat and red
vest.

My new friend from his earliest years had been
constantly on the stage. He played the gamin in
folk-scenes and the monster in burlesques. Besides, he was an adept at thunder and lightning;
by means of cracking a whip and the close imi-
tation of the neighing of horses, he announced the
approaching stage-coach; he lighted the moon in
" Der Freischütz "; and with a kettle and pair of
tongs gave forewarning of the witches' hour.
When I opened my heart to Lipp and confided to
him that I wanted to go on the stage, he reached
out his broad hand to me with emotion and said,
"And so· do I." Hereupon we swore eternal
friendship, and Lipp promised as soon as possible
to procure me an opportunity for putting my
dramatic qualifications to the test. From that
hour his manner changed towards me. Before,

he had treated me with some condescension, but now his behavior towards me was more like that of a colleague. Moreover, the game of chance for my lunch came to an end, for from that time forth I shared it with him like a brother.

The fine fellow kept his promise to make a way for me to go on the stage. A few evenings later (" Der Freischütz " was being played) I stood with a beating heart behind the scenes, and friend Lipp stood by my side. In my hand I held a string, with which I set the wings of the owl in the wolf's glen in rhythmic motion. My companion performed the wild chase. By turns he whistled through his fingers, cracked a whip, and imitated the yelping of the hounds. It was awfully fine.

" You did your part splendidly," said Lipp to me at the end of the scene; "next time you must go out on the stage."

I swam in a sea of delight. A short time after, "Preciosa" was given, and Lipp told me that I could play the gypsy boy. They put a white frock on me and wound red bands crosswise about my legs. Then a chorister took me by the hand and led me up and down the back of the stage two or three times. That was my first appearance.

It was also my last.   The affair became known. In school I received a severe reprimand, and in addition, as a consequence of the airy gypsy costume, a cold with a cough, which kept me in bed for a day or two.

"It serves you right," said Frau Eberlein. "He who will not hear must feel. This comes from playing in the theatre. If your blessed grandmother knew that you had been with play-actors she would turn in her grave."

Crushed and humiliated, I swallowed the various teas which my nurse steeped for me one after another. But with each cup I had to listen to an instructive story about the depravity of actors. In order to lead me back from the way of the transgressors to the path of virtue, Frau Eberlein painted with glowing colors; one story in particular, in which occurred three bottles of punch-essence never paid for, made a deep impression on me. But Frau Eberlein's anecdotes failed to make me change my resolves.

Soon after, something very serious happened. Lipp's father, the door-keeper of the theatre, after drinking heavily, fell down lifeless by the card table in the *White Horse;* and my friend, in consequence of this misfortune, came under the control of a cold-hearted guardian, who had as little comprehension of the dramatic art as Frau Eberlein. Lipp was given over to a house-painter, who, invested with extended authority, took the unfortunate fellow as an apprentice.

Lipp was inconsolable at the change in his lot. The smile disappeared from his face, and I too felt melancholy when I saw him going along the street in his paint-bespattered clothes, the picture of despair.

One day I met the poor fellow outside the city gate, where the last houses stand, painting a garden fence with an arsenic-green color. "My good friend," he said, with a melancholy smile, "I cannot give you my hand, for there is paint on it; but we are just the same as ever." Then he spoke of his disappointed hopes. "But," he continued, "because they are deferred, they are not put off forever, and these clouds" (by this he referred to his present apprenticeship as painter) "will pass away. The time will come — I say no more about it; but the time will come." Here Lipp stopped speaking and dipped his brush in the paint pot, for his master was coming around the corner of the house.

One day Lipp disappeared. The authorities

did everything in their power to find him, but in
vain; and since, at that time, the river, on which
the city stood, had overflowed its banks, it was
decided that Lipp had perished. The only person who did not share in this opinion was my
self. I had a firm conviction that he had gone
out into the wide world to seek his fortune, and
that some day he would turn up again as a celebrated artist and a successful man. But year
after year passed by and nothing was heard of
Lipp.

I had entered upon my fifteenth year, was
reading Virgil and Xenophon, and could enume-
rate the causes which brought the Roman empire
to ruin. But in the midst of my classical studies,
I did not lose sight of the real aim of my life,
the dramatic art; and as the stage had been
closed to me since my first appearance, I studied
in my own room the rôles in which I hoped to
shine later. Then I had already tried my skill
as a dramatic author, and in my writing-desk
lay concealed a finished tragedy. It was entitled " Pharaoh." In it occurred the seven plagues
of Egypt and the miracles of Moses; but Pharaoh's destruction in the Red Sea formed the
finale from which I promised myself the most
brilliant success.

Therefore I went about dressed as a regular artist. My schoolmates imitated the University students, — wore gay-colored caps, dark golden-red bands, and carried canes adorned with tassels; but I wore over my wild hair a pointed Calabrian hat, around my neck a loose silk handkerchief fastened together in an artistic knot, and in unpleasant weather a cloak, the red-lined corner of which I threw picturesquely over my left shoulder.

In this attire I went about in my native town, where I was accustomed to spend my summer vacations. The boys on the street made sport of me by their words and actions, but I thought, "What does the moon care when the dog bays at her!" and holding my head high, I walked past the scoffers.

Every year, in the month of August, a fair was held in the little town. On the common, tents and arbors were put up, where beer and sausages were furnished. Further entertainment was provided in the way of rope-dancers, jugglers, a Punch-and-Judy show, fortune-tellers, monstrosities, wax figures, and tragedies.

As a spoiled city youth, I considered it decidedly beneath my dignity to take part in the

people's merrymaking; but I couldn't get out of
it, and so I went with my parents and brothers
and sisters to the opening of the festival out in
the park, and walked more proudly than ever
under my Calabrian hat.

The sights were inspected one after another,
and in the evening we all sat together in the
front row of a booth, the proprietor of which
promised to exhibit the most extraordinary thing
that had ever been seen.

The spectacle was divided into three parts.
In the first a little horse with a large head was
brought out, which answered any questions asked
him by nodding, shaking, and beating his hoofs.
In the second part two trained hares performed
their tricks. With their forelegs they beat the
drum, fired off pistols, and in the "Battle with
the Hounds," they put to flight a whining terrier.

The proprietor had kept the best of all, —
that is, the Egyptian fire-eater, called "Phos-
phorus," — for the last part. The curtain went
up for the third time, and on the stage, in fan-
tastic scarlet dress, with a burning torch in his
left hand, there stood a tall — ah! a form only
too well known to me. It was Lipp, who had
been looked upon as dead.

I saw how the unfortunate fellow with a smile put a lump of burning pitch in his mouth, and then everything began to swim around me, I pulled my hat down over my eyes, made my way through the crowd howling their applause, and staggered home exhausted.

During the rest of the festival I kept myself in strict seclusion. I announced that I was not well, and this was really no untruth, for I was very miserable. "That is because he is growing," said my anxious mother; and I assented, and swallowed submissively the family remedies which she brought to me.

At last the fair was over, and the Egyptian fire-eater had left the town. But the poor fellow did not go far. In the city where he exhibited his skill he was recognized and arrested, because he had avoided service in the army. To be sure, he was set free again after a few weeks as unqualified; but in the mean time his employer with the performing hares had gone nobody knew where, and Lipp was left solely dependent on his art, which he practised for some time in the neighboring towns and villages.

The end of his artistic career is sad and melancholy. He fell a victim to his calling.

As an ambitious man he enlarged his artistic capabilities; he ate not only pitch but also pieces of broken glass, and an indigestible lamp-chimney was the cause of his destruction.

When I returned to the city I burned my tragedy of "Pharoah," and sold my cloak and Calabrian hat to an old-clothes dealer. I was thoroughly disgusted with the career of an artist, and whenever afterwards I was inclined to re-lapse, Frau Eberlein would call out to me, " Do you, too, want to die from a lamp-chimney?" Then I would bend my head and bury my nose in my Greek grammar.

THE WITCHING-STONE.

GAY banners were waving from the tower of the count's castle, and from the surrounding villages re-echoed the sound of merry bells. Joy had come to be a guest within the castle walls, and both bond and free in that domain rejoiced in its coming.

The young countess had given birth to an heir. The little lord was healthy and finely formed, made the walls resound with his strong voice, and vigorously kicked his feet, till his father's eyes shone with delight.

The day after his birth, when the child was taken to be baptized, the count dipped deeply into his treasure chest; all the servants received holiday clothes, and the poor in the land loudly praised their master's generosity. Then it became quiet in the castle. The boy lay peacefully in his nurse's arms, and his mother, Frau Gotelind, looked from her couch with a proud, blissful smile at the thriving child. She was a delicate lady, and her strength came back slowly; but it came, thanks to careful nursing and the appetizing broths made for her by old Crescenz.

She was a wise-woman, and well skilled in caring for the sick. Therefore the count had called her to the castle and intrusted to her the nursing of his wife. But the servants shook their heads thoughtfully when the old woman came in, for what people said of her was not good. Huntsmen and messengers had often met her in the moonlit wood, looking for herbs, and it was rumored that she could conjure up storms and dry the cows' milk. Therefore the men-servants and maids timidly avoided her, but scrupulously followed the orders which she gave.

Frau Crescenz was sitting in the kitchen, paring vegetables. Near her stood her daughter Ortrun, whom she had brought with her to the castle, that she might help her in her work. The daughter was a tall, well-developed woman, with raven-black hair, but her forehead was low, and her nose as flat as a negro's. She had killed and plucked a chicken to make some strengthening broth for the countess, and was just cleaning it.

"Look, mother," she cried suddenly; "see what is in the chicken's crop; he had swallowed a stone."

"Let me see," said old Crescenz, with curiosity, and Ortrun handed what she had found to her mother. It was a white, sparkling stone, shaped like a bean.

"Oh, you lucky child!" cried the mother; "that is a jewel more precious than a carbuncle or a diamond." Then she looked anxiously about her, fearing lest a third person might have been watching them, but, besides the two women, there was nobody in the kitchen.

"Dearest daughter," continued the old woman, — and her eyes shone like cats' eyes, — "the stone will bring you good luck. Keep your mouth shut and tell no human being anything about the chicken's stone. Conceal it well in your waist and guard it as the apple of your eye. The magic which the jewel contains will soon appear. And go to your room and put on your holiday gown; to-day you shall carry to the count his morning drink."

* * *

Where the deadly nightshade grows, there flowers of noble birth must fade away.

The countess had long since recovered, but she went about sadly, with downcast eyes. Her husband's love had gone out in a night like a candle burnt to the end, and she knew, too, who had caused the sudden change. The dark Ortrun, who, by her husband's command, had been made her stewardess, had captivated the count. She carried her head high, and gave commands boldly in the house, as though she were the mistress. Frau Gotelind sat silent and grieving in her chamber by the side of her little son's cradle, and at night her pillow was wet with tears. But when the nurse gently reproved her, saying, " My lady, you will harm the child if you look at him with sorrowful eyes," then the unhappy woman would compel herself to smile, and would sing in a low voice to the little one the old cradle song of the white and the black sheep. Thus passed a year of sorrow to the countess. But the boy thrived, and became a beautiful, sturdy child.

One day his nurse was sitting with the little one in the castle garden, the boy was playing in the grass with a small wooden horse, and his mother was standing on the balcony and delighting in the sight of him. Suddenly the child rose and stood for the first time on his feet, and made an unaided attempt to step forward. Just then the stewardess Urtrun came along, and the boy bent toward her, and seeking a support, grasped a fold of her dress with his little hand. The maid gave the child a push with her foot, so that he fell on his back with a scream, and went on her way scolding.

When the mother saw how the bold woman maltreated her child, her heart was convulsed with bitter anguish; but she was silent. She hastened down into the garden to her son, and soothed him with caresses. Then she sent the nurse under a pretext into the house, took the little one up, and, unnoticed, left the garden and the castle.

The countess and child were not missed till just as darkness was coming on. The count was much alarmed and sent out servants with torches to look for them in every direction. He himself mounted a horse and rode at random about the country. But master and servants returned without having found the lost ones.

The search was kept up for two or three days longer; then the count put on mourning, and hung a black flag from the tower.

It was supposed that the countess and her
child had become the prey of some wild beast
in the forest. The maid Ortrun and her wicked
mother carried their heads higher than ever, and
the old woman said to the young one: "It is a
good thing that she has gone off with her brat
of her own free will; otherwise — " But she
said no more.

A short time after Ortrun took possession of
the state-chamber of the vanished countess, and
it was as good as decided that at the end of the
year of mourning the count would make the
stewardess his wife. But when the year was
over, and the count wished to be married, the
priest refused to unite the pair, because it was
not proved that the countess was dead. So the
count had the name of her who had disappeared
posted up on the doors of three churches. Then
after another year, if no news came about her,
she might be considered as dead, according to
the laws of the country, and the widower might
take another wife. The second year too was drawing to an end, and nobody had heard anything
from the lost wife.

* * *

But the countess was not dead, and her little

son too was still alive. When, overcome by ex-
cessive grief, she had secretly left the castle, she
had wandered off into the wild forest, not knowing
where she was going. She walked the whole night
long, carrying the sleeping child in her arms. Occasionally the eyes of a wolf shone out of the darkness of the firs, but it did the poor mother no harm.
Towards morning, when the chilly wind blew
through the trees, her tender feet, unused to travelling, would carry her no farther. She sank down
on the wood moss and wept bitterly; now for the
first time she realized that she had doomed herself
and her child to destruction.

Then there suddenly stood before the desperate
mother a very old man, whose snow-white beard
from his face fell down like a waterfall. In his
right hand he carried a staff; in his left a bundle
of herbs.

The old man was a pious hermit, who had
turned his back on the turmoil of the world and
dwelt in the wilderness. He gave mother and
child some food, and led them to his hermitage.
The countess felt confidence in the hermit and
told him who she was and why she had taken
flight. And the old man comforted her and said,
"Stay with me, and share with me my poverty."

So the countess and her child remained with the hermit. By means of a wall of wicker-work he divided his hut into two rooms, and prepared a couch of wood moss and soft fur for his guests. For food he gave them goat's milk and whatever the woods afforded of berries, roots, and wild fruits. The life in the green forest agreed with the boy; he grew, and his limbs became strong and supple. The countess' ·delicate frame, too, became stronger; but her heart was still filled with a secret grief, for she could not forget her husband, and thought of him day and night. Thus passed nearly two years.

* * *

One morning the little one was jumping about in the forest and playing with a hazel switch, when the hoarse cry of a raven fell on his ear; and when he went toward the sound, he saw on the ground a flock of the black birds, who were attacking one of the number with their bills. When the boy ran toward them, the ravens flew away; but the one whom they had treated so badly could not lift himself into the air, but hopped painfully about on the ground, so that it was easy for the child to catch the bird. As he held his prisoner in his hand, he saw an arrow sticking in one of his wings.

He removed it and carried the raven home. The hermit, who was skilled in the art of healing, put a salve on the wound, and the little one cared for the sick bird very faithfully; and child and raven became great friends.

After some days the bird was well again, and when he felt that his power to fly had been restored, he flapped his wings with a croak, flew out at the door, and alighted on a bough not far from the hut. The boy did not wish to lose the raven, and ran after him to catch him; but just as he thought he was going to seize the fugitive, he escaped from him, and the play continued till it grew dark, and the raven disappeared in the shadow of the trees. Now the child wanted to turn back home, but he had long since lost the hermit's hut from sight, and did not know which way to turn. And he sat down under a tree and cried and called his mother, and he was hungry too.

Suddenly the raven appeared again. He carried a piece of bread in his bill, and dropped it in front of the child. Then the little one was half comforted, ate, and fell asleep.

The next morning he was awakened by the croaking of his companion; he arose and followed

the bird who flew before him, for he hoped he
would lead him back to the hermitage. But the
wise raven had a very different design. After
some hours of wearisome wandering, the forest
began to grow light, and before the boy lay a
shining castle, from the tower of which waved
a gay banner. It was the castle in which he had
been born, but he did not know it.

The raven had disappeared, but the tired little
fellow went up to the castle and sat down under
a linden-tree near the gateway. The keeper with
spear and helmet stepped up to him, and asked
who he was, where he had come from, and what
he wanted ; but he could get no information. The
servants gathered about the child, but they could
learn nothing from him except that he came out
of the forest, was hungry, and wished that he
was with his mother again. Then out of com-
passion they gave him food and drink, and
went about their work. The servants had plenty
to do, for on the next day the count was to be
married to the swarthy Ortrun.

The little one sat under the linden-tree and
ate the food which had been brought to him.
Then he heard the sound of wings. He looked
up and saw the raven hovering above his head;

he carried something that glistened in his bill,
and now he let it fall into his lap. It was a
fine gold chain from which hung a white, sparkling stone shaped like a bean. The boy examined
the shining ornament with curiosity, and finally
hid it in his dress. When the raven saw this he
croaked with delight, and flew up to the pinnacle
of the tower.

* * *

In the women's apartments there was a great
commotion. The count's bride was behaving as
though she had lost her mind, and at the same
time old Crescenz was scolding at the top of her
voice. Ortrun had been taking a bath, and when
she went to dress herself again, the magical chick-
en-stone had disappeared.

"Help me, mother!" cried Ortrun, in the
greatest distress; "help me, so that at the last
moment everything will not go to pieces."

"Help me!" said the old woman mockingly.
"Did I not tell you to guard the stone as the
apple of your eye? I decoyed the bird to the
lime-pole for you; keeping him was your affair,
you silly, heedless girl!"

The daughter stamped her foot. "You shall
help me!" she snarled. "Make use of your arts

and brew me a love-potion!   What is the good of
your being a witch?"

The mother's eyes shone green.   She gave a
leap, fastened her fingers in her daughter's black
hair, and threw her on the floor.   "A witch, am
I, you wicked vixen?   That is the thanks I get
for giving you a love-charm!"

She stopped abruptly, for in the open doorway
stood the count.   He looked as pale as death.

"Woman, what do you say about love-
charms?" he cried.

The women both trembled like aspen-leaves.
The count, moreover, threatened them with his
sword, and swore he would strike them to the
ground unless they confessed.   Then they threw
themselves on the floor before him, begging for
mercy, and acknowledged what they had done.

And the count looked with loathing and horror
at the woman who had ensnared him with magic
art, and the charming form of the wife whom
he had betrayed arose before him.   He groaned
aloud like a wounded stag, turned, and went out.

The two women collected together as many
of the jewels and splendid garments as they
could carry, wrapt themselves in their cloaks,
and fled from the castle like two gray spectres.

* * *

At the very moment when the charm over the count was broken, bitter repentance and a yearning for what he had lost filled his heart. In order to banish his tormenting thoughts, he ordered his horse saddled, and took his hunting-gear to hunt in the forest. As he rode out at the gate, his eyes fell on the lost boy sitting under the linden-tree, and he felt a stab in his heart, for he thought of his little son who would be about the same age as the strange child if the wolves had not torn him to pieces. He drew up his horse, and looked at the child, and an irresistible power compelled him to jump from his saddle and caress the boy. And the boy threw his arms about the count's neck and besought him in a tender, childish voice : —

"Take me back to my mother!"

"Where is your mother?" asked the count.

"There!" said the boy, pointing with his finger toward the fir forest.

Then the raven came, and croaking, circled round the father and his son. And the boy cried : —

"There is the bird that led me here; he knows the way to my mother." And the raven

screamed "Krah!" and flew toward the forest;
then sat down and turned his wise head towards
those he had left behind him.

Then the count said: "We will try to find
your mother," lifted the child on his horse,
and rode into the fir woods.   And the raven
flew ahead of them.

* * *

In the hermit's hut there was great distress.
All one night and all one day Frau Gotelind and
the hermit had searched in the forest for the
lost child, and at evening they both returned
from different directions without him.   The poor
mother wrung her hands in despair, and the old
hermit tried in vain to speak some comforting
words.

Then they heard the croaking of a raven and
the sound of hoofs, and Frau Gotelind hastened
out of the hut in anxious expectation.   A stately
knight came leaping along, holding on the saddle
in front of him the lost child.

"Mother!" cried the boy, still at a distance,
stretching out his little arms.   Frau Gotelind
was about to hurry towards him, but she trembled so that she was obliged to hold on to the
door-post, for the rider was well known to her.

The count reined in his snorting steed, sprang down, and set the child on the ground. Then he turned his eyes towards the trembling lady, and with a loud cry threw himself down at her feet. She flung her arms about her husband's neck, and clung to him laughing and crying.

The sun had gone to rest, and the bright moon was wandering through the fir forest. By the hearth-fire in the hermitage sat the count and his wife, as happy as a bride and groom who have just been united.

Then the boy, who had been a long time with the raven, came running to his mother, and laid the little chain, from which hung the white stone, in her lap.

"Where did you get this ornament?" asked the mother.

"The raven gave it to me when I was sitting in front of the castle, under the tree."

The hermit looked at the stone, took it in his hand, examined it closely, and said: —

"It is the Alectorius stone, of whose power old wise people tell wonderful things. It grows in a cock's crop, and fastens the man with magic power to the woman who wears the jewel concealed about her person. Believe me, my daughter, this stone has been the cause of your sorrow."

Then the count seized the chain, threw it on the floor, and raised his foot in order to crush the Alectorius stone.   But the raven was too quick for him, snatched the chain with his bill, and flew out of the window with it.   Whether he carried the ornament to his nest to enjoy its brilliancy, or whether he tried the stone's magic power on some coy raven damsel, the one who relates this tale has never been able to find out.

THE CHRISTMAS ROSE.

SCHNEEWITCHEN, wrapped in white sheets, was asleep in her glassy coffin, and the cold, wicked step-mother ruled in the land. She is terrible in her fury, but when she has her good days, and lets her diamond crown shine benignantly in the sun, then mortals may venture to approach her ice-palace unmolested. She has innumerable castles, but the most beautiful one stands on the Hochgebirg, and there she prefers to hold her court. The primeval mountains stand like venerable court-marshalls, with stiff necks and powdered wigs, around the throne, on which the queen sits, and the nixies of the mountain lakes, like trembling waiting-maids, hold the crystal mirror before their exacting mistress. She looks at her snow-white face and says: "I am the most beautiful in all the land," and not one among the people of the court dares to dissent.

Others think and speak otherwise. The blue titmice, and the golden pheasants who, hungry and cold, hop through the snow-covered branches of the fir-trees, chirping low, tell about the king's son, who will waken the sleeping Schneewitchen with a kiss; the rude raven croaks disrespectfully about the wicked queen, and the gypsy tribe of sparrows give vent to their discontent in loud abuse. The little brown wren who creeps through the dry bushes like a mouse, sings a mocking song about the severe mistress. He has made a discovery in the forest path. On yonder slope, where the mid-day sun eats up the snow, there is already a sign of life. Last night the Christmas rose broke through the sparkling covering, and with bended head greets the rising sun.

Do you know the Christmas rose? In flat countries it never grows, but among the mountains it is known to every child. In some places it is the snow-rose, in others hellebore, and it is called the Christmas rose because it blooms about Yule-tide. Its open calyx, which is about as large as the hundred-leafed rose, is snow-white, sometimes overspread with a delicate red, like a mountain snow-field at sunset;

and one unacquainted with the blossom's native soil would take it for the child of some far-off zone, so wonderfully beautiful it is. But the snow-rose has beside a virtue of its own, and whoever would know its origin must pay attention.

In a fruitful Alpine valley, through which a river fed with the milk of the glaciers rolled its foaming waters, there stood on a hill in ancient times a castle with a tower and encircling walls. Farther down on the river pious monks had built a cloister, and between the castle and the monastery lay a farm. To-day the castle lies in ruins, the monastery still stands, and the farm has grown in the course of time to a market town.

It was near Christmas-time, many, many years ago, and it was even more lonely and silent in the valley than usual, for all who could carry sword and lance had gone with the count, to whom the castle and land belonged, across the mountains to Italy.

The farmer too, as one of the count's people, had been obliged to leave his home; and although he was always ready for battle, yet this time his going away was very hard, for he had to leave behind him a blooming young wife and a little three-year-old girl.

The Christmas festival was at hand. In the
hall of the farmhouse the hearth-fire was crackling, and busy maids in linen aprons were mix-
ing and kneading the dough for the holiday
sweetcakes. Frau Walpurga, the mistress of
the household, was not present. She was sitting
with her heart heavy with anxiety by the bed
of her child who was restlessly tossing about
her little head burning with fever. On the opposite side of the sick-bed stood a monk with
a shining bald crown and gray beard. It was
Father Celestin from the monastery, a pious
man, experienced in the art of healing. He
scrutinized the sick child, shook his head, and
began to mix a drink from the medicines he
had brought with him.

Heavy footsteps were heard outside in the
hall, and an old man, wearing a mantle of coarse
material, entered the sick-room; in his left hand
he held a broad-brimmed hat, and in his right,
a lamb carved out of wood. The man was the
shepherd of the farm. He looked darkly at the
monk, then stepped up to the little bed, and
held the lamb before the child. He had made
two coal-black eyes for it with pine soot, and
with the juice of berries, a red mouth; but the

child did not notice the plaything. The mother
sighed, and the shepherd left the room as quietly as he could. The monk gave the healing
drink to the child, spoke some words of com-
fort, and went out. Mother and child were alone.

The physician's remedy seemed to do good to
the feverish little girl. She fell into a deep sleep,
and slept all day. But as the sun was going down,
the child grew restless again; her forehead burned
like fire, and she spoke incoherent words. All
of a sudden the little one lifted herself from her
pillow and said: " See, mother, see the beautiful lady and all the little children, and the lady
gives me roses, white roses! " Then she fell
back again, and closed her eyes. But Frau Walpurga knelt down, sobbing softly. — " The child
has seen the angels of heaven; she must die."

The mother did not long give way to her distress. She hastened to the door, and called the
servants to send a messenger for Father Celestin. But both men-servants and maids had all
gone to the monastery church to hear the Christmas service. Only one old lame woman had been
left behind to tend the hearth-fire. Frau Walpurga commanded her to put out the fire, and
stay by the child. She wrapped her cloak about

her, left the house, and went in all haste to the
monastery.

The sun had already set: only the mountain
tops still gleamed a ruddy gold; in the valley the
twilight had spread her gray garment of mist
over the snow-fields. No living creature was
to be seen, except two rooks flying towards the
forest, slowly flapping their wings. In the far
distance a light flickered through the mist; it
came from the lighted windows of the monastery church; and the mother, with her heart
full of anguish, hastened over the creaking snow
in the direction of the light.

Suddenly her feet stopped, and her breath
failed her. Out of the forest came a long procession of misty forms, led by a beautiful, tall,
serious lady, in a broad, full cloak, and behind
her tripped a crowd of little children with pale
faces, clad in white.

The trembling mother concealed herself behind the trunk of a tree, and let the procession
pass by. At the very end came a child who
could hardly follow the others, for she was constantly stepping on her dress, which dragged on
the ground. Then Frau Walpurga forgot her
distress, and overcame her dread. She stepped

toward the child, and tucked up her little frock
so that she could keep pace with the other children.

And the beautiful pale lady turned her face
toward the helper, smiled at her, and pointed
with her forefinger to the ground at her feet.

At this moment the sound of monastery bells
trembled through the air, the procession disappeared like mist scattered by the wind, and
Frau Walpurga stood in the twilight alone on
the snow-covered plain.

With timid steps she approached the spot to
which the woman had pointed, and her heart
leaped for joy. Out of the ice-covered earth was
growing a bush, bearing green leaves and white
roses.

"Those are the roses my child saw in her
dream!" exclaimed Frau Walpurga; then she
plucked three of the blossoms, and hurried as
fast as she could go back to the farmhouse.

Besides the maid she found the old shepherd
by the sick-bed. He had little regard for the
skill of the monks, and therefore he himself had
made a drink out of goat's gall and juniper berries, and had given it to the little sick girl.

Frau Walpurga stepped up to the bed, laid

the three roses on the spread, and watched the child with anxious expectation. She seized the flowers with her little, trembling hands, held them to her face, and sneezed loud and strong.

"God bless her!" cried mother, shepherd, and maid. Then the child asked for a drink, turned her head on one side, and fell asleep.

"Now the fever is broken," said the shepherd. "My drink and the sneeze have saved the child. But where did you get those roses, Frau?"

Frau Walpurga quietly told the old man what had happened to her.

"That was none other than Frau Berchta with the cricket folk," explained the shepherd. "She wanders about every evening from Christmas till Twelfth Night, and my father has seen them too. Formerly she dwelt up in the Frauenstein, but when the monks built their house of stone she departed, and only shows herself during the twelve nights after Christmas, and blesses the land. It was lucky for you, Frau Walpurga, that you helped the cricket. Frau Berchta is a gentle lady, and rewards every service that has been rendered her." And then the old shepherd told what he knew about Frau Berchta, and he would have talked on till the cocks crowed, if Frau Walpurga had not brought him out of the sick-room with friendly words.

Once more she was sitting alone by her child's bed. The little one held the three roses in her closed hand, and she breathed peacefully and easily. Only once she murmured in her sleep, when the sound of the organ and the monks' song of praise, *Gloria in Excelsis*, were heard from the monastery. And the mother knelt down and was long at prayer.

When Father Celestin came the next day to see the sick child she was sitting up in bed, playing with the lamb which the shepherd had carved for her.

"Frau Walpurga," said the delighted physician, "the fever has disappeared. But it was a costly drink that I prepared for the child. I hope you will show your gratitude to the monastery."

But Frau Walpurga drew the monk aside and told him confidentially what had befallen her on Christmas Eve.

The Father knit his brow. "You were dreaming," he said, "or else the snow blinded your eyes. Take good care that none of your idle talk comes to the ears of our abbot; it might cost you a heavy

penance." But when Frau Walpurga showed him
the marvellous roses, the like of which the botani-
cal doctor had never seen before, he grew thoughtful, and he finally said : —

"Woman, you have been highly favored. You
have with your bodily eyes beheld the Queen of
Heaven and the blessed angels in her company.
Our Dear Lady it was who gave you the three roses,
the mother of our Lord, and not the dreadful
sorceress, whose name no Christian may bring to
his lips. Be assured of that, woman. And now
listen to me further. The Madonna above the
side-altar in our church is in need of a new robe
as well as a crown. Show your gratitude to the
mother of God, and provide her with new apparel.
Will you promise me that?"

And Frau Walpurga, frightened by the monk's
warning, said, "Yes, it shall be as you wish."

Thereupon she had a side of bacon, two fat
geese, a pot of lard, and a bottle of red wine placed
in a basket, and ordered a maid to take it and
follow after Father Celestin to the monastery.
And Father Celestin, with a smirk, blessed mother
and child, servants and house, and went away, followed by the panting maid. But the old shepherd
muttered to himself, "There again, one carries

away the thanks which belong to another"; and by "another" he meant himself.

Frau Walpurga thought the same, but she said nothing. She gave the shepherd a handsome present; and the Madonna in the monastery received a silver crown and a new robe, on which lace and spangles were not used sparingly.

But the flower which grew up in the footprints of the heavenly queen — or was it, after all, Frau Berchta? — bore seeds and multiplied in the land, and according to trustworthy witnesses has in later times worked many a miracle.

THE MATCH-MAKERS.

THE sun, after a short course, was about to
go to rest. It tried to gild the spires and
the snow-covered gable roofs, and as it was not
remarkably successful in this to-day, it sank
hastily behind a gray cloud. Stars here and
there peeped out at their windows, but the
mist, rolling up from the mountains, spoiled
their view, so they closed their windows again
and went to sleep. Besides, their glimmer this
evening was superfluous, for in an hour thousands and thousands of lights, kindled by
happy mortals, would shine through the De-
cember night. Christmas, the merry time, had
come, and a multitude of visible angels, bringing joy, were crowding the streets and alleys
of the old city.

Beings of flesh and bone, and cheeks rosy
with the frost, were also hurrying through the
streets. Most of them carried some carefully

wrapped object, which later, when it lay beneath the brightly lighted fir-tree, would be greeted with a cry of joy. Everything was in haste to-night. No groups of gossiping servants hindered the stream of passers-by, and if two people happened to recognize one another, they hurried past with a hasty greeting. Little by little it became more quiet on the street, the shop doors were closed, and the windows in the dwelling-houses grew bright. Here and there the muffled shouts of the children came forth from the houses, and the watchmen with echoing footsteps paced the pavements.

Through the door of an old patrician house entered a tall man, wearing a broad-brimmed hat and a long cloak. A white poodle followed him. Having reached the second story, the man opened a door, the plate of which bore the name of a celebrated artist, and after a few moments he entered a comfortable room, illuminated by soft lamp-light. A huge gray cat rose from her cushion which lay near the stove, and with a low purr greeted her master as he entered. Then she showed the same politeness to the poodle, and laid herself down again. Poodle and pussy had known each other for many years, and lived together, not like "cats and dogs," but like two excellent chums who have been together at school.

The man took off his hat and cloak, and went to the window. In the opposite house flickered the lights of a Christmas tree, and the shadows of the children and grown-people stood out on the lowered shades. The man looked at the lighted window for a long time, then turned away, brushed his hand across his eyes, and said softly to himself, "I am alone."

The poodle, as if he would have liked to contradict this, approached him, and rubbed his cold nose against his hand; but his master paid no attention to the caress. "I am alone," he repeated. Then he sat down in his easy-chair, and fixed his eyes on the floor.

No bright pictures were they which passed before the lonely man's mind : — a melancholy childhood, a youth full of cruel privations, wearisome struggling and disenchantments of every sort. Honor and wealth had at last fallen to his share, but in the time of need he had forgotten how to enjoy himself. Youth was past; in his dark hair the frost of early autumn already shimmered, — and he was alone.

Then, as he sat thus brooding over the past, he suddenly heard close to him the words: "Old friend, shall we chat together? The master is asleep."

"I am willing," came the answer. "You begin."

"That is my poodle and my cat," said the man to himself, "and I am dreaming. To be sure, on Christmas eve, animals have the power of speech; I used often to hear that when I was young. If only I do not wake up before I learn what the two have to say to one another!"

"Friend Pussy," the poodle began, "do you know that for some time the master has not quite pleased me? He has neglected me. I will forgive him for not having me sheared in the summer, but it hurts me deeply that he almost never claims my services."

"Yes," replied the cat, "he is no longer as he used to be. Just think, yesterday he even forgot to give me my breakfast. At last I shall have to return to my former life of catching mice. That would be hard."

"Do you know, my dear," said the poodle, "what would be the best thing for us and

for him? If we had a woman in the house
who would look after our rights and keep things
in order."

"Oh!" exclaimed the cat, "that is a doubtful
suggestion. The wife would probably look on
the friends of her husband's youth with dis-
approval. We have both seen our best days.
Suppose the young woman should show us the
door, what then, brother?"

"But I know one who would not do that,"
replied the poodle, " and you know her too."

The cat pointed with her fore-paw to a little
picture on the wall. It was a woman's head
with large, dark, childlike eyes. "Do you mean
that one there?"

"Yes," said the poodle. "She would be the
woman for us. She is friendly toward me,
that I know; and she doesn't dislike you, for
I have seen with my own eyes how lately, when
you creep around her window, looking for
sparrows, she sets out a cup of milk for you.
And our master—"

"She likes him too," said the cat, filling out
the sentence. "That I know; for when she is
sitting by the window, sewing, and the master
passes along on the street, she turns her pretty

white neck after him, and blushes. And when people blush — "

" I know what that means," interrupted the poodle. " We are both agreed, and that is the main point. She must be our mistress."

" But the master ? " asked the cat, doubtfully.

" That will be all right," said the poodle, confidently. " But hush ! He is moving ; he is waking up."

The sleeper leaped from his chair, and looked suspiciously at his companions. But they lay, to all appearance lost in sweet dreams, curled up like snail-shells on their cushions, and never stirred. And with his hands behind his back, the man strode up and down the room, like one who is striving to settle some weighty question.

Let us leave the solitary man, with his poodle and cat, and mount the stairs as far as they go, — and they reach to the roof, under which, in narrow chambers, poor, worried people rest from their day's labor. In one of these little rooms, — the cleanest and neatest of all, — sat two women, one old, the other young. Before them on a table stood two smoking

cups and a cake cut in pieces. The maiden
had a delicate, pale face, and two large dark
eyes, which looked out into the world sometimes merry and sometimes sad. The young
girl was a seamstress; the old woman a laun-
dress by trade, and the younger one's aunt.
She had come from her damp home in the
suburbs to receive the presents which her niece
intended for her: two or three pounds of
sugar and coffee and a knitted hood of soft
gray wool, which the old woman stroked from
time to time caressingly with her wrinkled
hand. The cake on the table grew perceptibly
smaller, for the aunt ate as though she had
fasted for three days; and when she could
take no more, she, after some resistance, allowed the seamstress to wrap the rest in paper
to take away with her.

"Child," said the old woman, as she was
getting ready to go home, "you would be wise
to go to sleep early this evening, for in the
holy Christmas night all sorts of strange things
happen, — and you are so entirely alone! Don't
you feel at all afraid?"

The maiden shook her head with a laugh.
"What sort of strange things, auntie?"

"Did you ever pass by a church at twelve
o'clock on Christmas eve?" asked the laun-
dress. "No? Oh, if I should tell you! But
I will not make you timid. A maiden can
learn, too, on Christmas eve, who will be her
husband; but that is a dangerous story."

The little one pricked up her ears. "What
must one do to find out that?" she asked.

"Child," said the old woman, warningly,
"you will not try it?"

"No, I am not so inquisitive; but I should
like to know how one must go to work to find
it out."

The aunt sat down again and began to dis-
play her wisdom. "If a maiden sits all sole
alone in her room on Christmas eve, and lays
the table for two, her future husband will appear to her. But he has no flesh and blood;
it is an apparition, and vanishes when the
cock crows. Therefore the maid would do well
to have a cock near her in a bag. And if
the uncanny guest should cause her to be
afraid, she would only have to pinch the cock;
then he would cry out, and the ghost would
disappear. Many say it is the Evil One who
assumes the form of the lover. I do not really

believe that, but it is a dangerous game, at
any rate.   I went through terrible suffering
when I tried the trick."

"Really?" asked the maiden, with curiosity.
"Did you try the magic yourself?   And did
somebody come to you?"

"No," said the old woman; "nobody came,
and so I knew that I should be an old maid;
and that I really am.   But it troubles me
sorely to think I have told you all this.
Truly, you will not try it?   Well now, my
child, thank you very much for the Christmas
gifts, and hold the light for me, for it's as
dark as pitch outside, and the stairs are so
steep."

The seamstress accompanied the old woman
with the lamp, and then went back to her
silent room.   The hot drink had made her
little face glow, and as she busied herself in a
matronly way, putting the plates and dishes in
their places, she would have been a charming
sight for anybody's eyes; but there was no
one who could refresh himself with a look at
the young blossom.

What her aunt had been telling her went
round and round in her head.   At first she

laughed at the Christmas magic, then she grew
thoughtful, and finally — it was surely only a
harmless joke — she brought out a white cloth,
spread it on the table, and laid it for two.
There, now he can come. To be sure, she
had no cock, but she wore a little cross around
her neck, and every sort of ghost must vanish
before the cross. She sat down, folded her
little hands in her lap, and called up to mind
the men whom she knew, — the curly-haired
shopkeeper in the grocery shop, who always
weighed out the sugar and coffee for her so
generously; the sergeant, who occasionally met
her and greeted her so respectfully; and the
writer in the house opposite, who played on
his flute every evening "If I were a bird,"
— but none of these was the right one. At
last she came to one more, but he was a
serious, fine gentleman, who could hardly remember the poor seamstress in the garret.

Two years before, when her mother was still
living, he met her for the first time on the
stairs, had stopped and looked at her with the
most gentle eyes. On the following day he had
spoken to her, and asked her to sit for him
as a model for a picture. At first she had

objected, for she had heard horrible stories
about painters and models; but the gentleman
had spoken so courteously to her! And so
she went, accompanied by her mother, to his
studio. Afterward she had seen the finished
picture too. It represented an old man with a
harp, and by his side sat a young girl, and
the young girl was the little seamstress — her
very self. When the picture had gone out into
the world, the painter had placed a large bank-
note in her work-basket. She had really not
wished to take it, but as her mother then lay
on her death-bed she did not dare to return
the gift, and the money went just far enough
to bury her mother and to get a little cast-
iron cross for her grave. She had never
spoken to the painter since that time, but she
saw the serious man every day, and she had
formed a friendship with his two companions,
— a poodle and a pussy-cat, — and was kind
to the animals whenever she had an opportunity.

The lamp blazed up and started her out of
her dreams. She saw the two plates before
her, and she smiled, and then gave a sigh.
" You are a thoroughly silly creature," she

said softly, and rose to put away the dishes
again.

Then there came a knock at the door.
Heaven help us, if the Christmas magic is
really no fairy tale! And the door opened,
and the apparition which appeared in the
doorway was like the painter to a dot. The
poor little girl sank trembling into her chair,
and hid her face in her hands.

"Good evening," said the ghost in a deep
voice; and then he came nearer, sat down by
the seamstress, and took her hand. Ghosts
usually have ice-cold hands, but the one which
grasped the trembling maiden's was full of warm
life.

And then the ghost began to speak. He spoke
of the lonely, joyless existence he led, and then
many other things about love and fidelity, and
the maiden listened with a beating heart. If he
were no ghost after all! With trembling hands
she felt for the little cross she wore in her waist.
Before the cross all magic is destroyed. She
drew it forth and held it before the ghost.

But he smiled, seized the cross, and said:
"Poor child, you do not believe my words. I
swear to you on the cross which I hold in my

hands that I am true and honest in my intentions toward you. Will you be my wife?"

Then the little one's soul rejoiced like a lark.
No, it was no apparition to vanish into mist
at the crowing of a cock; it was one of Adam's
sons, with flesh and bone. His mouth, which
her lips sought, was warm, and his heart beat
violently against her breast.

O blessed, merry Christmas!

Then there was a scratching at the door, and
when it was opened the poodle came in with
a bound, and behind him was seen the cat.
They came to bring their congratulations. The
poodle jumped up, now on his master and then
on the maiden, whining for joy. The cat arched
her back, and purred like a spinning-wheel.
That the two people had found each other was
the work of the wise creatures. They were
proud of it, but said nothing about it, for true
merit is rewarded in silence.

A HAPPY MARRIAGE.

A CONVENTION of magicians was to be
held in Africa, and guests came to the fes
tival from all quarters of the globe in aerial con
veyances. Among others, an aged fairy had left
her castle, and undertaken the journey. Her
dragon-coach in the course of years had become
somewhat decayed, and as it was coming down a
steep cloud-mountain the axle-tree broke. The
coach immediately began to fall, and whirled,
together with the struggling dragons, down to
the solid earth. A fairy can endure more than
mortals, but still she was very much alarmed at
the accident, and the fact that she landed directly
in the midst of a populous town considerably increased her anxiety.

The city was none other than Simpel, and the
people who surrounded the shattered coach were
Simpletons. How they opened their eyes! Emperors and kings had often been entertained

within their walls, but a fairy who journeyed
through the air with a team of dragons they had
never yet beheld. However, they conducted themselves like brave Christian people. The coach
they dragged to the blacksmith's shop, they put
the dragons in the stable, and filled the crib with
pitch wreaths and brimstone matches. But the
burgomaster invited the fairy in appropriate language to come to his humble dwelling and take a
lunch to recover herself from the fright she had
undergone.

The fairy accepted the gallant man's invita-
tion, refreshed herself with food and drink, and
later the burgomaster took her to see the sights of
the city. Then, indeed, she saw many things that
she had to shake her head over, and what she
learned about the customs and doings of the
people made her very thoughtful. When she
returned to her host's house again, she took her
magic book in her hand, and soon knew all that
she wanted to know. " The worthy people must
be helped," she said to herself, and asked the burgomaster to grant her an interview.

At first she praised the city, and then began
cautiously to draw his attention to the existing
poverty and crime; and when the consul, shrug

ging his shoulders, admitted that things were
really not altogether as they ought to be, the
fairy said: "Gracious, burgomaster! A fiend
has established himself in your city, and for hun-
dreds of years has darkened the minds of the cit-
izens, and — pardon me — yours as well. But I
know how to exorcise spirits, and will free your
city from the plague if you will accompany me
to the court-house."

So they went together to the windowless court-
house, which was lighted with miserable oil
lamps. There the fairy opened her book and
began the exorcism. She had been whispering
her magic words for a good while, when all of a
sudden the door of the large oaken cupboard, in
which the city seal, the chronicle, and the most
important documents were kept, opened with a
great creaking, and bluish smoke began to pour
out from the inside. The burgomaster fortified
himself behind a chair, and awaited the appearance of the spirit with fear and trembling. But
the fairy continued her exorcism, the cloud became
condensed, and finally the spirit assumed bodily
form. It did not excite fear and dread, but rather
pity, for it appeared like a young woman with low
brow and delicate features. And the maiden, or

whatever it was, immediately began to weep and sob, as if her heart would break.

"There is your city ghost," said the fairy. "Now try your best to get rid of her. But do the little creature no harm. You must promise me that."

The burgomaster had found his courage again. He looked at the pitiful form, and then asked her sternly, "Who are you?"

But the maid could give no answer, for she was sobbing so. Then the fairy bent towards the burgomaster and whispered a word in his ear, and the honorable gentleman fell back alarmed into a chair. "Horrible!" he groaned, and buried his face in his hands. Thus he sat for a long time.

"Make an end of it, good burgomaster," said the fairy after a while, "and send her away."

"Yes, she must go," said the disquieted official. "She shall go unharmed from here, but she must swear that she will never come back again."

She did so. Then the burgomaster gave the exile a pass, and furnished it with a seal and an illegible signature, and when the vesper bell sounded the evil spirit had already left the city far behind her.

* * *

Sadly went the banished spirit along the country road. She journeyed all night long, and when the awakening birds became noisy, and the mountain-tops began to grow rosy, she came to a village. She dimly remembered having once lived among the peasants, and that she did not have a bad time then. Therefore she made up her mind to try her luck in the village.

By a gurgling well stood a handsome peasant woman with red arms, pouring water into the milk that she was going to carry to the city. The woman was Country Simplicity. The pilgrim timidly approached her, and asked in a shy voice, " Possibly you are in want of a maid ? "

" A maid I certainly am in need of," replied the peasant woman, and looked the stranger criti-cally in the eye. "Oho, it's you, is it?" she ex-claimed, and burst into a loud laugh. " I know you ; I have often seen you in the city. No, my good girl, there is no room for you in the village. Go on further ! " And Country Simplicity turned her back on the poor creature, and went on with her work.

The maid continued her way. She went from house to house, but she was welcome nowhere ; they ·turned her rudely or scornfully from the

door, and the dogs barked after her. The same
thing happened to her in the next town, and she
had begun to look about for a corner where she
could stay at night, when she happened on an old
gloomy house, whose door stood carelessly open.
She went in, and found in an arched room on the
ground floor an old woman busily writing by the
light of a lamp. Dusty books and gilded parch-
ments lay about everywhere, and spiders had spun
their webs in every corner. The woman who was
writing was Knowledge.

" Do you need a maid?" asked the outlaw in a
low voice.

Knowledge pushed her horn spectacles upon
her forehead, and inspected the stranger; nodded
her gray head with satisfaction, and said : " There
is something about you that pleases me. You can
remain." And the stranger remained.

It was not a difficult position to be in the service of Knowledge, and the mistress grew daily
more fond of the industrious, quiet maid. Occasionally, when she was in a particularly good
humor, she would read a passage from her manuscript to the servant, and ask, " What do you
think of that?" Then the maid would answer
and give her opinion as well as she could, and

the dame would nod an assent, and write down the maid's words on the edge as a gloss. It was a fortunate union.

But one day a man came to the house who had orders from the king to write down the names of all the people in the city, — men, women, and chil-- dren, — for the king wished to know how many sub- jects he had. So the maid was brought out to the official.

"Have you a certificate or anything in writing to show where you belong?" he asked; and the maid produced her passport that the burgomaster of Simpel had given her. The man looked at it with astonishment, then handed the paper to the mistress of the house, and asked with a laugh, "Do you know whom you have taken into your house?"

Knowledge took the passport, read it, and let the paper fall from her hands. "Oh my good- ness!" she groaned in an undertone. Then she implored the officer not to say anything about it, paid the trembling maid the wages due her, gave her some cast-off garments besides, and bolted the door behind the departing bird of misfortune.

* * *

With hanging head the poor thing crept out of the city; and when, after a hard journey, she reached a wood, she decided to live in it and become a hermit.

She had spent several days in the wilderness, when one morning, while gathering berries, she came to a garden fence. Strange trees and flowers grew in it, and birds of shining plumage sang in the branches. An old woman was taking a walk along the path strewn with golden sand. She was none other than the fairy who had driven the unfortunate creature into banishment; and as soon as the maid recognized her enemy, she fell on the ground with a loud scream.

The fairy came to the fainting girl, lifted her up, and gave her some strengthening balsam. Then she led her, trembling, into her castle, and quieted her with friendly words. "You may stay here," she said, "for a few days, and rest yourself. In the mean time, I hope that just the right thing will be found for you. I am to blame for your misfortune, and it is right that I should help you out of it."

Hereupon the fairy shut herself up in her study, and called up the spirits that served her, to hold counsel with them.

On the third day the fairy sent for the little stranger. She looked very friendly, and said: "My child, I have something good in store for you. In a short time your sadness will be changed to joy." She rang for her waiting-maids, and ordered them to dress her charge in costly garments. The waiting-maids did their best, and when, after an hour, the stranger in her adornment appeared again before her patron, the fairy nodded her head in approval. "Come, and follow me!" she said, and conducted the little one into the courtyard. There stood a dainty, milk-white ass, provided with wings, and a woman's saddle. "Mount!" commanded the fairy, and helped the maiden into the saddle. Then she whispered something in the ass's ear, and the ass gave a joyful bray, lifted his wings, and rose like a falcon into the air. "Hold on fast!" cried the fairy, and waved her handkerchief. The winged ass had soon mounted so high with his burden that he looked no bigger than a lark above the cornfields. But the fairy, smiling, rubbed her hands with satisfaction.

The magic ass understood flying. He shot straight ahead like a dove striving to reach her own dove-cote, and when he saw his goal lying beneath him, he sank very slowly down, that his rider might come gently to the ground.

The ass stopped before a magnificent castle; the coat of arms above the door showed a golden turkey on a red field. Gaily clad servants rushed forward to assist the extraordinary rider from the saddle. At the foot of the broad marble steps stood a dignified man, gorgeously dressed, who was the lord of the castle.

Graciously he took off his hat adorned with ostrich feathers before the stranger, and led her into the interior of the palace. Oh, what magnificence!

When they reached the drawing-room the lord dropped politely on one knee before the lady, and said: "Be welcome, charming fairy child! Know that I am immortal, and only an immortal can become my wife. Therefore fate has led you to me. I am Pride." He rose and stood in all his magnificence before the stupefied girl. "And who art thou, my adorable angel?" asked Pride. "What is thy name?"

The stranger lifted her face, and tears were shining in her watery blue eyes. "Ah," she sighed, "I dare not deceive you. Immortal I

am indeed; but if you should hear my name
you would drive me from you. I am — "

" Why do you hesitate, heavenly fairy?
Speak! Who are you?"

"I am Stupidity," stammered the lady, and
held her hand before her eyes.

The lord of the castle laughed till the arches
rang. "And do you think I believe that?"
he cried. "Never! But you shall be called
whatever you please. I will nevermore let you
leave my side, and the wedding shall be this
very day. Are you willing?"

Then Stupidity with a beaming face fell on
Pride's decorated breast, and whispered, bliss-
fully smiling, "Yes."

Above them the ceiling of the drawing-room
opened, and in a rosy cloud appeared the good
fairy and blessed the union of the happy pair.

www.ingramcontent.com/pod-product-compliance
Lightning Source LLC
Chambersburg PA
CBHW030957260626
47169CB00002B/578